NORTH
BY
2000

a collection of canadian science fiction

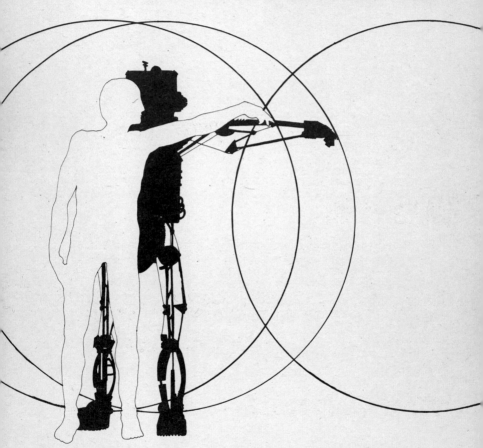

NORTH BY 2000

H.A. Hargreaves

H. G. Hargreaves

Peter Martin Associates

Canadian Cataloguing in Publication Data

Hargreaves, Henry A., 1928 –
  North by 2000

ISBN 0-88778-128-4 pa.

1. Science fiction, Canadian (English).
I. Title.

PS8565.A735N6 1976   C813'.08'76   C76-017005-3
PR9199.3.H3N6 1976

© 1975 H. A. Hargreaves
  paperback edition 1976

Design: Tim Wynne-Jones

PETER MARTIN ASSOCIATES LIMITED
35 Britain Street, Toronto, Canada M5A 1R7

United Kingdom: Books Canada, 1 Bedford Road, London N2, England.
United States: Books Canada, 33 East Tupper St., Buffalo, N.Y. 14203.

These stories have appeared previously in the following publications:

"Tee Vee Man", *New Worlds* vol. 46, no. 137 (December 1963), 60-71; *Lambda I and other Stories,* Penguin Books Ltd., London, 1965, 57-70; (as) "El Hombre de la television", *Lambda I y otros relatos,* Barcelona, 1967, 6177.

"Dead to the World", *New Writings in SF 11,* Dobson—cl, Corgi—pb, London, 1968, 139-156; *New Writings in SF 8,* Bantam, New York, 1971, 125-142.

"More Things in Heaven and Earth", *New Writings in SF 17,* Dobson—cl, Corgi—pb, London, 1970, 11-66.

"CAIN[n]", *New Writings in SF 20,* Dobson—cl, Corgi—pb, London, 1972, 83-134.

"Tangled Web", *New Writings in SF 21,* Sidgwick and Jackson Limited—cl, 1972, Corgi—pb, 1973, London, 117-145.

Dedicated to my children
whose evolving struggles with
ethical problems
keep me optimistic.

Contents

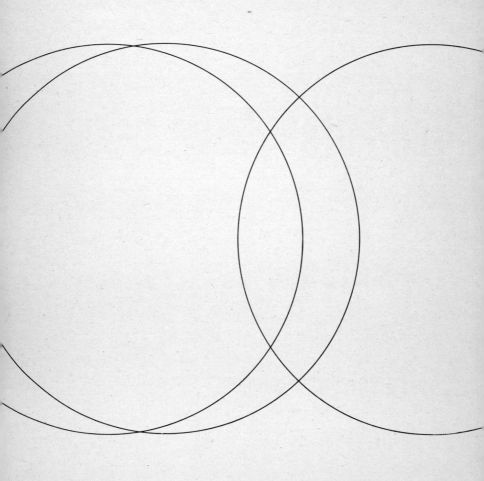

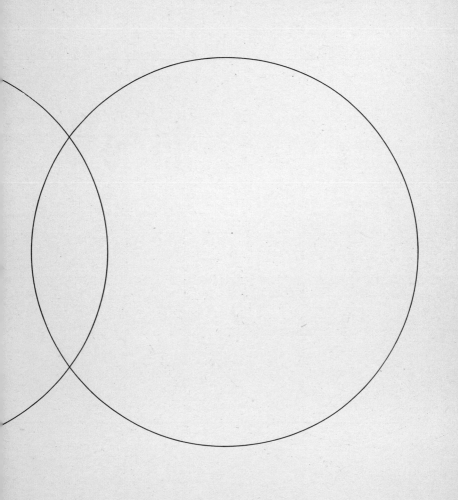

rld he W ad

1

Dead to the World

1

In the murmuring voice of a thousand quiet sounds, the great machine sang softly to itself; a never-ceasing, contented sort of song, sentient, and somehow self contained. It sprawled beneath innumerable acres just on the outskirts of the once-small city of Rugby, North Dakota. Through its myriad channels, like blood through a human body, two hundred and fifty million cards moved swiftly, surely, momentarily caught here to receive an electronic notation, passing elsewhere to be relieved of that notation. In a hospital in Indianapolis a baby was born, placed before a scanner, touched briefly by tendrils at head, chest, wrist and ankle. A new card appeared in the smaller machine beneath that great city, to be duplicated an instant later at Rugby. IN97246-IND38452 had been incorporated into the population of Americanada, had received her permanent ID card, and no matter what name she might be given by her parents, no matter what her friends might call her, no matter what husband she might choose, she would remain to the machines, those recorders, masters and manipulators of vital statistics, all sixty-five of them if required, as IN97246IND38452.

In Saskatoon, Saskatchewan, a police robot picked up one male, adult, from the prone position into which he had fallen, carried him through the crowd to the cruiser at the curb, and after a cursory examination fished an ID card from the body's pocket, passed it through a scanner, and made a report. In machine number fifty-eight, about fifty miles north of that metropolis, card SA537SAS8442 was flicked into a side channel, passed beneath several recorders, and dropped at last into a receptacle marked Deceased, stilled for the first time in several years. Again, an instant later, card SA537SAS8442 was sidetracked in the machine at Rugby, to drop eventually into a similar receptacle. This time, however, the one-in-a-hundred-million possibility discounted by technicians and authorities came to pass. As the card was flicked into the side channel a minute variation in current caused an "echo", and the card behind was flicked in too. So it happened that LA96647ONT374699 came to rest, and shortly thereafter at London, Ontario, the duplicate did likewise — Deceased.

In Lambeth, Ontario, it was one of a lifetime of identical days for everyone, including Joe Schultz. Having finished his work at the antique furniture plant, Joe had decided that he wanted the company of an autoteria rather than the drab silence of his bachelor roomette. Prices being the same whether you slipped your ID card into the slot at home or at the autoteria, the main difference was that you could see the actual rows of offerings rather than mere pictures, and there was life, such as it might be, around you. Moreover, there were opportunities for an enterprising man like Joe. He had punched his choices, picked them up at the robo-cashier's desk, and noted with some discomfort that his receipt was blue, though it was still nearly a week till "pay day" rolled around. Well, he thought, often enough he was on the red by this time, and had once or twice even had to go through the lengthy routine of securing extra credit to be placed against his account a few days before pay day. And he was one of the fortunate ones: he actually performed physical work of a certain specialty, thereby gaining a little higher credit in his account. (Let no one ask how he had got the job.) He wondered how others could survive as mere button pushers.

Joe looked carefully at the diners, finally choosing one somewhat overweight, middle-aged woman who sat alone with her tray of calory-rich foods. Slipping deftly between tables, he came to a firm stop, flashed a brief smile, said "May I?" and sat solidly opposite her. For the first moment or so he concentrated on the fairly meagre contents of his own tray, ignoring the faint but insidious background music which was psychologically designed to speed up the act of eating, to move more people through the place each hour. Then he began to size up his table companion, the "target", in order to plan his brief campaign. She was obviously unaffected by the music. A tough case for his purpose, but this made it more of a challenge. As an opening gambit, he deliberately pushed aside some of his greasy french-fried potatoes, clucking softly to himself. He caught a flicker of interest in the woman's eye, a hint of surprise, and it was all too easy after that.

"Keelosterole," he said to his companion, stabbing with his fork at a pale-green snap bean. "You know," he added, as the woman's brow furrowed with concentration, "gets the insides of your arteries." He went back to worrying the contents of his plate for a moment. Then, just as her attention was about to shift away from him, he flashed a rueful grin at the woman. "Had a buddy go that way last year, so I'm touchy on the subject. Nice guy he was, though. Big, happy, healthy, he looked, until the day he . . . went. Hardened up arteries, the Doc said. Yes, sir. Heart couldn't take it, you know. Doc warned him. He said leave those calories alone, and those fat foods . . . they're poison. Nothin' but poison. Old Art wouldn't listen, though. Nice guy, he was."

Joe subsided, just barely watching out of the corner of his eye as the woman's mouth went hard and straight. Then she shrugged her shoulders and picked up her fork. Joe shoved his half-empty plate away and lit up a cigarette, watching the news-fax as its words crawled across the far wall. The woman paused, fork halfway to her mouth. She took a mouthful of food. Slowly her fork came down, dropped to her plate as she sighed, pushed back her chair and heaved herself up. Only after she had left the restaurant did Joe slip her dessert onto his tray, finish his own meal in leisurely fashion and savour his prize. It had been easy after all.

Feeling as much at peace with the world as he ever did, Joe decided that his little victory warranted an extra cup of coffee, sidled over to the beverage area in a mood of self-congratulation, and slid his ID card into the slot. For a fraction of a second it failed to register on him that his cup remained empty, that in fact the machine had rejected his card. Puzzled, he looked at card, cup and machine, then tried again. Again the machine dropped his card into the rejection tray. Joe stood in complete amazement, trying to think out what might be wrong, only moving away when the line behind him began to grow restive. Such a thing had only happened to him once before, and then he had been given sufficient warning from his red receipts but had chosen not to ask for advance credit until he actually ran out. But he knew the simple meal he had bought just now could not have run him completely through the blue and onto the red.

Shaking his head, he moved down to the end of the service spaces, to a slot with a malevolent red light over it, and a sign which read Official Enquiries. After a moment of hesitation he slipped his card into the slot and waited. The hum of scanning equipment stopped, but the machine retained his card for what seemed an agonizing length of time. Finally, with a kind of hiccough, the card was released, and from a special slot at the side there issued an instruction sheet. Joe pulled the sheet free and read with mounting incredulity:

NOTICE: The card you have found belonged to a person now deceased. Please deposit it in the nearest Government Incinerator chute, labelled Official Documents.

WARNING: It is a legal offence to retain the ID card of any person deceased. A record of this enquiry has been preserved, and action will be initiated if the accompanying ID card is not destroyed within 48 hours.

Aware now that something had gone drastically wrong with his "records", Joe was quite uneasy, but still, his mind told him, it must be relatively easy to straighten this out. He knew that occasionally something went wrong, and he had heard of people who had run into problems larger than mere overspending. There was the legend of the guy who had been billed for something like one hundred times his expected life earnings, though. Seems, Joe mused, that he was made president of something so he could pay it off. That's right — he was made president of the foreign country whose loan had been placed against his account. Well, at least his own next step was clear. He would have to find a written enquiry booth, fill out a form and get this straightened out quick. Suiting action to thought, he left the autoteria and headed for the local government building.

Half an hour later, Joe Schultz, deceased, was on the walkway again, shaking his head in utter disbelief. He had tried three different forms, none of which seemed precisely to fit his case, each one being returned by the machine with the identical notice and warning he had first received. Finally, in desperation, he had filled out a form requesting information on persons deceased and received a sheet directing him to his nearest Coroner's Office or an accredited spiritual advisor. With this sheet still clutched in his hand, he returned slowly towards his apartment block, painfully attempting to make some sense out of the situation. But more complications were still to come. On arriving at his own door, he found a pair of robo-movers meticulously cleaning up after having removed all his personal belongings and the one or two pieces of furniture that he had purchased over the past few years.

It was too much. In a burst of anger, Joe stepped in front of one of the movers and wrenched the polishing cloth out of its grasp.

"Whatta you tryin' to do?" he shouted at the machine. It simply stood still, waiting, humming to itself, while the second machine, obviously more complex, turned and moved swiftly up to him. Scanners moved up and down briefly, another sheet of paper was ejected at Joe, and both machines went back to work. Helplessly, he stood and read the directions for "Next-of-kin", which advised him that his goods had been removed under seal to a government warehouse, pending issue of redirection orders, and warning him that it was a felony to attempt to remove any article, or to impede, obstruct, or in any way to interfere with the work of the robo-mover. Now totally confused, Joe wandered aimlessly from the building and down the walkway trying to understand what had happened to him in so brief a time, and to think of something, anything, he could do next.

The Coroner's Office, his first sheet had said. But it would be closed now, he realized, and moreover if it was like the few offices he had been in there would be a robo-clerk anyway. He watched the faces of the few people moving purposefully along the walkway, wondering idly if any of them had ever run into such a problem. It would do no more good to ask for help from any of them than it would to drop onto one of the motorways far beneath him, with its unceasing flow of muted thunder. You lived your own life, these days, and the fewer questions asked the better. Stop that burly guy there, for example, and ask him for help, he thought. Looks like the kind who would set you up for the hospital first, and find out later if you were trying to heist him.

"The hospital," Joe said aloud. That might be the answer. At least temporarily. He had been in hospital twice in his life, and each time it had been a very pleasant experience. Lots of rest, good food, even some nice-looking girls around, though they didn't have time to talk to ordinary patients. He could stand that, all right, at least for the night. Of course, if they stuck him in the analyzer he might get thrown out, but the second time he'd been admitted they hadn't examined him till the next morning. He remembered being pretty riled up over that, thinking at the time that he might die before they got around to finding out what was wrong with him. And he'd felt pretty foolish the next day when they told him he'd just had too much of a bad batch of Alkade down at the Lambeth Auto-Bar. At least it was worth the chance that they would admit him tonight, before they found out he was faking. "Nineteen-hundred right now," he mused. "Can't take a flipper anyway, if I can't pay the fare, so if I walk it will

be 19:30 when I get there. I'll wait till 20:00 and then try to get in."
He felt a bit better now that his mind was functioning again, though
he still wasn't sure what he'd do next day. He set out towards the
hospital, mulling over possibilities.

The little park in front of the hospital was pleasant, one of the
newer models ingeniously designed to provide an illusion of isolation
almost immediately one entered it. It took a sharp eye to determine
which of the shrubs, trees and flowers were synthetics at this time of
year, when everything was determined to grow, no matter what the
odds. Joe noticed that the grass had recently been replaced: there was
one spot where the manufacturer hadn't got enough green into it. In
all, though, the effect came through, and he began to relax a bit for
the first time since his card had been rejected. It was almost dusk
when the robo-watchman arrived and the concealed air rejuvenators
had begun to hum, before he decided to try his luck at the admittance
entrance.

Taking a deep breath, he stepped slowly through the doors and up
to the desk, where a slim and decidedly junior staff member was
busily stacking punched cards. In a hoarse and, he hoped, sick-sounding
voice, he gave his name and asked to be admitted. The girl straightened up, faced him, and asked, "Could you give me some idea of what
the, uh, nature of your complaint is?"

Joe had already thought this out in the park, and now he looked
down at the floor, shuffled a little, looked at the back wall of the
office and muttered, "Well, Miss, I'd rather tell a doctor. But it hurts
a lot, a lot, you understand. If I have to . . . I could wait a little . . . "
He let his voice trail off and shuddered slightly.

"I'll let you go to one of the emergency stalls," the girl said quickly,
"and send an intern as soon as possible."

"Thanks," Joe said between gritted teeth. "Which way is it?"

"Down this hall to your left," the girl answered, and as he turned
to leave she continued, "You have your ID card with you, of course."

"Sure," Joe said, fishing it out and holding it up in front of the
desk while she rose as if to glance at it. Then, faster than he could
have anticipated, she reached out and took it from him, held it between trim thumb and forefinger, and slipped it into the admissions
machine. Numbly, Joe stood waiting, not sure of what might happen
next, but certain that something would. It did.

While the girl watched, horrified, two light-green robo-attendants
moved swiftly and silently to a stop, wheeled stretcher between them.

Before she could do anything to prevent it, they had picked up a sub-missive Joe, slipped him onto the stretcher, strapped him down and headed back down the hall. Joe had no idea of where he was going, but he was fairly sure it wasn't to an emergency stall. He was deftly wheeled into an elevator, plummeted into the depths of the building, and just as deftly wheeled out into a subterranean corridor.

In front of a door labelled *Morgue* they stopped for a brief second, and as it opened soundlessly Joe suddenly realized what had happened. He was paralyzed with fear as the robo-attendants lined him up with toes pointing towards a bank of overlarge drawers. One of the ma-chines opened the drawer as the other efficiently loosened the straps. Without really thinking, Joe sat bolt upright, slipped around the attendant, and made for the end of the bank of drawers. Looking back over his shoulder, he caught a glimpse of the two robo-attendants moving in futile circles, searching the floor for their missing body. Then the door opened in front of him and he was through it, into the corridor, and leaning weakly against the wall.

Summoning up his strength, Joe headed back to the elevator, punched the button and glanced feverishly over the floor list beside it. "Walkway Admissions—35", he read, and as the elevator door slid back he whipped in and punched 35. Breathing deeply as the car ascended, he tried to slow his racing pulse. Then, moving quickly without actually running, he retraced his path. Ahead, the little girl, as white now as her uniform, was explaining to a full-fledged nurse, waving his ID card to give emphasis. Breaking into a run, Joe passed between them, grabbing his card on the way. Only when he was across the walkway and into the park did he stop, slump-ing down onto a bench to seek for calmness after his narrow escape.

The robo-watchman had passed twice, and was standing unobtru-sively but warily in the shadows of a Manchurian elm down the path, before Joe had collected his wits sufficiently to consider his next move. Hospitals were out. The Coroner's Office was closed. His "accredited spiritual advisor" seemed like the only remaining hope, and here there was a small problem. He had never had even a nodding acquaintance with a spiritual advisor, though he knew they existed in some sort of continental association to whose advertising he had been exposed.

Trying hard to remember the name of the association, he went quickly back across the street, down the express escalator till he came to a visitor's entrance, and cautiously moved through the hospital lobby to a seetalk booth. Thumbing the scanner for the Yellow P., he watched racing capitals until *S* appeared, then hit the mid-speed until *Sp* came up, and switched to slow until *Spiritual Advisors* showed. "Christian Unitarian Spiritual Society" was second in a short list that began with "Buddhist Friends Society". Scanner reversed, he moved at high speed back to the *C* range, stopping at CUSS. It took a short time to find the address of his nearest advisor, the list again containing fewer names than he had expected. He was about to place his call when he realized that he could no longer do so, since one had to present his ID card even for a collect call. Instead, he memorized the address and took to the walkway yet again, happy to be doing something to keep his mind from being paralyzed by creeping hysteria. Within fifteen minutes he was standing before the sub-level apartment door of Benjamin Scroop, B.A., M.A., B.D., Ph.D., D.D., Spiritual Advisor.

Scroop, Joe quickly learned, was a man who clearly gave far more attention to the needs of the spirit than the body. He stood about six-five, weighed about one-sixty, and had huge, wistful brown eyes that looked from a distance like chocolate mints adrift in a bowl of instant milk. Eager to be of help, he invited Joe to step in and unburden himself, and Joe accepted. It was incredible, Joe thought, as he squeezed onto a thinly-upholstered bench at one side of a fold-down table, how much could be recessed into the walls of an Efficiency Living Space. He had read about the ELS in passing, but this was his first experience with one. Here were three rooms, counting bathroom, in a space smaller than his one-and-a-half. No door, of course, between this and the bedroom, where he could see three triple-tiered bunks folded up to the wall. Scroop answered his casual question with a rueful "Seven. Seven children, my wife and myself. The children seem to spend every waking minute at the House Centre, and my wife works. It's only crowded for breakfast, supper and sleeping."

Joe made an inane comment about not needing an office with such an arrangement, thinking all the while that in these surroundings a well-fed soul *would* be much more comfortable than a well-fed body. But it was time to get down to his problem, since he figured the rest of the family would be back pretty soon. Briefly he sketched out what had happened to him, and filled in details in response to precise questions from the extremely sharp Scroop. This character, Joe thought, might be a spiritual advisor, but he certainly seemed to know the shape of the hard world outside his door. He allowed himself a bit of hope.

But any optimism he might have generated was soon squelched by Scroop, who said quite frankly that in his dealings with the Coroner's Office he had gone through more foul-ups than straightforward situations. No more than two months ago they had, on the same day, cremated a Fleshly Resurrectionist, and mummified a Fiery Purger, both with relatives seeking Scroop's counsel. If anything, the robo-clerks were more to be trusted than the occasional human clerk, who invariably fed the wrong data into the larger machines. As for the chief coroner, he was in London Proper and Scroop had suspicions that he wasn't human either, since his decisions were arbitrary and calculated to inflict spiritual suffering on the living, if they could merely subject the dead to indignities. Joe commented that from his own knowledge of the world it sounded as if the chief coroner were all too human. However, he saw there would be little help in that direction, and asked if there were any other way Scroop could think of to get him out of his now-desperate situation.

Scroop could think of little more that might be done, and they were slowly discarding possibilities when, in quick succession, the rest of the Scroops arrived home for sleep. A few of the youngest wanted milk, and Joe, after much urging, accepted the cup of coffee he had tried to get so long ago. Well, it seemed ages ago, even if it was only five hours. Scroop used his Householder's ID Card, and Joe couldn't help but notice in such close quarters that the family was on the red. He felt an unaccustomed flush of guilt, as he realized how hard it must be to feed and clothe this mob. Scroop had seen his discomfort, however, and laughed a bit ruefully, trying to make Joe more at ease. "Don't worry about it," he said. "In this house it's the children who feed the rest of us, anyway."

Joe wasn't used to family life, but he knew that children didn't get all that much government allowance, so he raised an eyebrow. Scroop explained. "You see, all the money that people donate to our society is deducted from their accounts by the government. It's used first to cover land taxes and rent, next mission expenses, then operating expenses, and finally the rest is evenly distributed in salaries. I make about half as much in a month as one of my children gets in subsidy. But the children, bless them, believe in the work I do, so they have all, at age six, given up their personal allowance entirely to our household account. It's a rare display of faith in their parents on the part of youth, especially for these days." Joe was forced to agree. Things hadn't been so totally controlled by government until after he had left home, and he wondered if he would have consented to such a thing when he was a kid, considering the tough times his family had seen in the Soaring Sixties.

After the children and Mrs. Scroop had gone to bed, Joe and Scroop sat talking for a short time, but it was clear that there would be no solution here. Scroop promised to make out as many forms as he could think of that would be remotely related to Joe's case, but he did not hold out much hope for quick relief. He offered to put Joe up and feed him, and he was sincere, but he and Joe knew it was next to impossible under the circumstances. Without seeming to rush, Joe brought the talk to an end. "If I don't mosey along," he finally said, "my friend Max will've gone to bed. And he doesn't like to be woke up late at night. He gets real ugly. So thanks for everything, and I'll be dropping around sometime. I might even take in one of your services." After a firm handshake and a look of real compassion from Scroop, Joe found himself outside, heading for the blessed walkway, this time presumably to see the mythical Max, who, Joe decided, lived under a bench in the park across from the hospital.

Back in the park, with the time nearly a murky 24:00, Joe carefully chose a secluded nook surrounded by thick shrubs and overhung by an original Canadian maple. He had not realized how tired he was until he stretched out with his jacket under his head. Then, despite the turmoil of his thoughts as he tried to find some way out of his dilemma, he dropped into a deep, uneasy sleep. He dreamed of running down long, twisting corridors whose walls pulsed rhythmically, threatening to close on him. Paradoxically, it seemed that he could always see a dark abyss at the end, no matter what direction he tried. Then, dimly, he became aware of an insistent, toneless voice, and slowly roused to find the robo-watchman standing over him in the darkness of the park.

"It is forbidden to remain off the pathways after dark," the watchman repeated. Joe was stiff, incredibly tired and totally discouraged. He could think of nothing more to do, so he lay there in complete resignation.

"I will be forced to call for the police if you do not leave at once," said the watchman, and Joe thought, well, it had to come to this sooner or later. Then he brightened. Why not? Why not go to jail? At least he would have a place to sleep in peace, and maybe someone would straighten the whole thing out when his case came up. Of course, loitering must be a minor offence and he would be dealt with by machine again, but at worst he would merely stay in jail. He put his hands behind his head, relaxed and waited.

It couldn't have been more than three minutes later when the robo-cop arrived, moving swiftly and competently across the grass while his companion remained behind, at the cruiser. Joe had obligingly placed his ID card on his chest, and now he waited with grim satisfaction to be apprehended. But it didn't happen quite that way. After a quick glance, the robo-cop's tentacle flicked down and took his ID card, shoved it into its scanner, and transmitted the information. Joe watched with bewilderment as his card was placed back in his shirt pocket and the robo-cop stood still, obviously waiting. Then with a soft swoosh a "black hack" settled on the grass close by, two attendants got out with wheeled stretcher, placed him on it and wrapped him in a sheet, put him in the back of the vehicle and took off.

This time it was the District Morgue, but the procedure was precisely the same. As the sheet was unwrapped, Joe slipped off his stretcher and made for the door. Glancing back, he saw the attendants making those same futile searching movements in widening circles around the floor. It was somehow ludicrous now, as Joe made his way in leisurely fashion through the sub-basement area, not really caring where his wandering took him. It was almost pleasant down here, the warm, dim passage inviting him to find a little nook or cranny, curl up and finish his sleep. He had to make a real effort to keep going, realizing that this was no solution either: that he had to make his way to the outside, if only to eat. And now that the thought had occurred, he was acutely hungry. It must be early morning, at least.

O-five-thirty, said the clock over the back entrance to this level of the mammoth civic building. He knew he shouldn't really be so hungry, but Joe had been through a lot since supper the night before, and it definitely wasn't all psychological. He would have to find some way to get breakfast, and if it required desperate measures, well, it was a desperate situation. One or two meals he might go without, but he wasn't going to starve, even if it seemed that the "machine" was intent on having him dead to make the records accurate. He set out for an autoteria, still not quite sure of what his next move would be.

There was a big one only a block down, and Joe stood across from it watching the early-morning crowd scurry in and out. There was no use going in until he knew what he would do. He could try to force the serving doors, but he couldn't guarantee that they would pry open easily, and besides, there would be loads of people watching him. Not that it mattered much now, but he still wasn't ready to commit an open theft. No, there had to be a better way. What about a back entrance, he thought. It has to have a service area. He began to search, and before long found a neutral grey door marked *Food Services.* Gently, he tried the door, opening it slowly until it stood wide, revealing a small room with three more doors. One said *Accounts,* one said *Maintenance* and the third said *Unauthorized Persons Not Permitted.* Like the old stories on Kid-vid, he thought, in a flash of wild humour. Obviously it was the last that he wanted, and without further delay he opened it and passed through.

To his left a scanner blinked officiously at him, demanding that he present his ID card, but he was interested in the magnificent view that stretched in front of him. Racks of prepared plates lined one side, coming up on a conveyor belt from an escalator at the far end, while smaller belts moved endless amounts of food to the pigeon-holes where customers made their purchases. Entranced, Joe watched toast and jam, eggs, bacon and eggs, ham and eggs, pancakes, muffins, buns — enough for an orgy. Then, shaking his head as if hypnotized, he loaded himself down with pancakes, bacon and coffee. He reached across a belt and picked up knife and fork, seated himself on a stack of waiting trays, and began wolfing his meal. Halfway through the coffee, the robo-cop came. Joe stood still, licking syrup off his fingers, as the cop moved warily into the room blocking his escape. "Please do not move," said the cop, "or I will have to detain you by force." Joe reached for his coffee cup, and almost too fast to be seen the robo-cop pinned his arms to his sides. Another tentacle snaked out and checked his pockets, removing his ID card and inserting it in the scanner. At the same time, Joe felt himself being touched at head, chest, wrists and ankles; a procedure that had familiarity somewhere beyond the fringes of memory.

The robo-cop hummed as time spun out, and Joe began to sense that something was not going quite right. Gradually the hum increased, the robo-cop's visual sensors began to glow brighter, and it even seemed to Joe that the tentacle that held him grew tighter. Soon he could smell the odour of scorched insulation, and see tiny wisps of smoke issuing from minute fissures in the robo-cop's shell. At last, with a belch of smoke and a drunken lurch, the robo-cop disgorged his card, unrolled limp tentacles, and went dead. Amazed, Joe could only watch for a moment or so. He had never seen any piece of automated equipment do this before, particularly none with any degree of independent decision-making abilities. It was almost like watching a person die. He picked up his card half-expecting the cop to come to life and seize him again, but nothing happened. Regaining some composure, Joe moved cautiously to the belts, picked a slab of apple pie, and with studied disdain held it between thumb and fingers as he swaggered by the silent, burnt-out robo-cop. Only when he reached the outer room did he hurry.

It was 10:00, and Joe Schultz, deceased, was reclining in a luxurious bed, in one of the most luxurious hotels in the Greater London area. He had got there by the simple expedient of reaching across the end of the desk, behind the recepto-clerk, and taking one of the two keys in a slot nearest him. Check-out time was 14:00, European style, he knew from the high-priced ads following the newsfax. He might have seven hours of uninterrupted sleep, he figured, but if he were interrupted, so what? For Joe Schultz had found the solution to his problem. It had been right there in front of him all the time, if he had only stopped thinking like a good, law-abiding citizen. The real tip-off had come when the robo-cop, efficient law-enforcement officer that it was, had broken down under the onslaught of conflicting information. When it apprehended a moving, living law-breaker, it seized and identified both ID card and offender. Joe knew little about the information patterns of such machines, but he lay there in delight, imagining what had gone on. Offender carried card of Joe Schultz. Joe Schultz was deceased. Offender was identified therefore as . . . Joe Schultz. Joe Schultz was deceased. Offender was alive. Offender's card there identified him as . . . Joe Schultz. Pluooi! And if he preferred, he could always stay absolutely still, to be carted off to the morgue. He squirmed and stretched into a more comfortable position, drifting off into sleep as he envisioned the clothes he would secure, the foods he would eat, the places he would sleep. In the immense peace of the truly free, Joe Schultz lay, dead to the world.

2

Tangled Web

2

The perspective was rather surrealistic. From the edge of the apron a few yards ahead of him, an intricate web of plastic pipe, conduit and cable stretched outward across the permafrost to the perimeter of the townsite. It was bounded on one side by a finished subdivision and on the other by the two-hundred-foot razorback ridge thrusting up at right angles to the river. Arching overhead was a maze of temporary lattice, from which this service hardware was suspended, and high above that was the infinitely more complex, invisible web of SAC, endlessly whispering to the Artic sky. Some wag, he thought, must surely have worked out a name later to suit those initials. Supersonic Air Carapace, indeed! Well, it was a sac after all, meshed above and below to protect man from this hostile environment. Or were they still deceiving themselves? A Closed Environment set into the Arctic Protected Environment. Wasn't it Isaiah who had said, "The earth lies polluted under its inhabitants?"

He slouched against an untidy pile of wooden crating and watched while a spindly monster rolled slowly forward with high-pitched whine, trailing cable like some futuristic umbilical cord. As two men handed up bags from the side-bed, two more emptied them into the cooker and the operator lowered the long, wide-mouthed blower over the edge of the apron to lay a steady stream of foam. Three feet of Schlagge foam, the perfect insulator, shielding the permafrost, embedding the service hardware, making a grey-white, supertough floor for the homes in which the final one hundred and fifty families would live. But at least the interiors would have colourful laminates, a vital addition. He looked outward from under the latticework, through the

SAC shimmer, across the reach of rivermouth towards Welcome Sound and shivered slightly as his eyes strained to find where grey-white met white-grey in the fine haze of lifted snow.

Even where he stood, a few droplets sifted on to his silver hair, indicating that the new section of SAC was not completely meshed yet. He straightened his gaunt frame slowly, forcing ageing joints to measure his full six-foot-five. Flicking spray from his lowered hood he turned away from the construction area, where already men were dismantling the first section of lattice, stopping only to pull off a gauntlet and run his hand over the wood he had leaned against. When had he last felt wood, he wondered; even rough scrap like this. Crating. The extravagance of it made him painfully aware again that he was an alien here. The machines had been cradled in this, carried by tractor train on the ice of Hudson Bay (thus getting around the Protected Environment regulations) for hundreds of miles from the Quebec shore to this mining site, to get the construction done by break-up. The credits it had cost were too much for him to imagine. With a shrug and a pushing back of old shoulders, he moved off the growing apron and through the subdivision airscreen, into the comfortable five degrees Celsius of Tundra City's "main" street.

Stepping out in a deceptively unhurried pace, he returned to City Center, turning huge brown eyes up to the chrono mounted on the only third storey in town. Sixteen-twenty—plenty of time before his appointment with Vladmir Homynyk, and he was reluctant, as always, to go to his own quarters. He sauntered through the lobby, reading notices on the bulletin boards, passed the steps to the upstairs rec rooms and entered the barnlike gymnasium, cum cinema-theatre, cum ballroom—and church.

At the far end, next to the left stage entrance, was a flush plastic door with a sign: "Benjamin Scroop, Spiritual Advisor". Grimacing, Scroop visualized a third line: "Computerized Confessions", which was perhaps more appropriate in view of what he had accomplished here so far. Some seven hundred and fifty souls were entrusted to his care, in three splinter congregations and a sprinkling of other sects, and to an individual they seemed either engaged in insidious obstruction or totally inert. For the life of him he could not understand why he, with less than a year to mandatory retirement, should have been plucked from his parish in London, Ontario, and posted to a—a mine town. All Hail the Great God Computer, he muttered mutinously. Well this time the computer had erred, and the Placement Committee was either blind or senile to have accepted its recommendation. Yet in his heart he knew his self-deception and with a soul-sick acceptance he granted the computer its dispassionate accuracy.

He himself had spun the thread which led to this end many years ago. Schlitz, or something, he had called himself, the man who appeared one night at the Scroop ELS, asking for help which the spiritual advisor could not provide. The Continental Computer had somehow struck that man off as dead and so he was dead to the world, for all practical intents and purposes. Scroop had watched him go back out into the darkness, to cope alone with his dilemma, and after a sleepless night the scholarly cleric, with his earned D.D., had set aside his love for religious history and begun a new study. He would acquire the proper pastoral skills.

Now with ironic amusement he went into his "office" and private quarters which, unpartitioned, had previously been used to store gym apparatus. It was part of the general conspiracy to keep him uncomfortable, to let him know he was unwelcome. It was bad enough, with its unrelieved grey-white walls, ceiling, floor, its slapped-in fixtures and furnishings. But what these independent Old Canadians didn't realize was that he had more space here than in his Stretched Efficiency Living Space at home; vastly more than in the ELS of those many years ago, with a wife and seven children. Here, the old widower rattled like a pea in a dry pod. And he had the two vital tools of his trade hooked up and working, both the viewer-scanner and the remote access computer console. Theoretically, it should merely be a matter of time until he had his situation under control, drawing upon the resources of the Regional Computer and the library, in Winnipeg. Nevertheless, it was as if his familiar arch-enemy, the Continental Computer, while acknowledging him as a wily master technocrat, had named him for this task to show him what he had really lost on that night when he decided to meet his parishioners' world on its own terms.

Meanwhile, it was time to meet another master, Vladmir Homynyk, and as if on cue the chief steward of Local 764, Mining, Smelting, and Refining Union, appeared at Scroop's door. "Come in, come in," Scroop said mildly, "take a pew." He rolled his own chair past the corner of the scanner, into what might be called casual space between the equipment and the door, but Homynyk refused to descend to informality. Prowling restlessly through the cramped office, from door to partition setting off the tiny bed-sitter and back again, he turned abruptly and asked, "What is it this time? You got any more ideas that can't be done?" He placed a meaty hand on top of the computer console and smeared grime on to its hood from his thumb. (There had been ample time to wash and change after he left the pits.) Scroop built a steeple with long, pale fingers and looked over it with wistful brown eyes. "I'm afraid it's nothing new, Vladmir," he murmured, "just the same old question. As patriarch, when are you going to arrange for me to provide your congregation with daily religious instruction?"

Homynyk snorted, "You're wasting your time and mine. Religious instruction begins with the men, and you aren't qualified."

Scroop asked innocently, "And just once more, why am I not qualified?" In disgust Homynyk made as if to leave, but turned with undisguised scorn and levelled a forefinger.

"I told you a dozen times, we saw all this coming before I was born. When Old Canada and the U.S. incorporated. We ain't just Orthodox Ukrainians—we're unionists. The community don't just have any old Holy Joe. He's a priest and he's a card holder: a chaplain of the local. I told you to read the Union's Reformed Constitution." He wiped his nose with a hairy wrist, as Scroop rolled his chair back to the scanner and flipped the switch. "That's one of the things we got against you CUSS men," the steward finished. "You got all the answers under your switches, except the ones you need for a man's world."

"But I took your advice, Vladmir," Scroop offered quietly. "I flipped a switch and read the constitution. And I flipped it again and read the original constitution, because in some places the new one simply says 'as per the old'." Vladmir's eyes narrowed slightly and Scroop continued. "A spiritual advisor for the Christian United Spiritual Society is acceptable to all sects of the merged Christian faith, but he does have to meet local needs."

Vladmir's voice dripped scorn as he answered, "And we in Old Canada never merged. Regardless of the UN ruling on our petition, you don't belong. You don't qualify."

Scroop leaned back in his chair and sighed. "I was up at 04:00, Vladmir," he replied. "I went down to pithead 6 during the first shift. The foreman very kindly showed me how to operate the auger and I cut two feet of face. I rode an ore car up and helped couple it at the tunnel siding." Vladmir opened his mouth, but Scroop held up a hand. "I was over at the smelter at 10:00," he continued, "for a look-in. Got a chance to pry slag out of one furnace. Hot work, even in the suit. And last," he smiled faintly, "I was over at the refinery at 14:00. A docker let me put some ingots on the robofreight with his forklift." Vladmir moved back into the room and sank heavily into a chair. Scroop's smile became absolutely benign. "Yes, the original constitution must have had men like me in mind. And the second doesn't revise *that* section on chaplains one bit. I believe I've qualified three times over, don't you?"

Not that it really changed things, Scroop thought after Homynyk had left. The chief steward knew that he had seriously underestimated his rival. But it would be long and hard work till Scroop gained real acceptance with the congregation. The computer had given him a group profile of astonishing cohesion and identification with the patriarchal figure. There were, however, theological points on which he could develop his own roots within the congregation. One thing was certain: they were in desperate need of spiritual renewal and guidance. From him? His own soul-sickness rose again, but he consciously thrust it down. There was more work that he was peculiarly fitted to do and he had best be about it.

Henri LeBlanc preferred to work during the third shift and since he was the manager of the Hudson's Bay Company store, no one could argue, had anyone cared. Perhaps it was because even during the early summer, when it never really got dark, there was less business than during the other two shifts, hence he could take care of the light duties created by his second job as nominal mayor of Tundra City. He was in a mood apparently as expansive as his ample middle and greeted Scroop jovially enough. "Which hat shall I put on, Mr. S.A.?" he chuckled. "On what business do you come to my little shop?" Scroop glanced through the clear plastic to the main floor of the store below and lowered himself into a chair as if listening for squeaky hinges. "Henri, mon fils," he grunted, "it has nothing to do with your congregation—at the moment, though there are certain things which must soon cease upon pain of excommunication. Yours!" He watched as a shadow of fear flitted across the other's face, and then barked a short laugh. "Come," he said, "you were too good a student while you were at seminary to take me seriously. After a number of years one easily forgets things, or perhaps one may have left before acquiring certain knowledge. Such as who may give absolution, or extreme unction to the dying when an ordained priest is within call."

Henri's normally ruddy face went quite pale and Scroop pressed while he had the storeman on the defensive. "No, no," he waved a boney hand, "let us not speak of this unfortunate death for the moment. I come, rather, to speak for Christian charity. The matter of the sacramental wine. Not for myself, though I would prefer to consecrate official spirits for my daily communion. For the Anglicans, Henri!" He added just a hint of pleading to his voice. "They have not taken communion for years, some of them, because the congregation has not had a priest, yet now they refuse because the wine is not official."

Somewhat relieved, Henri threw up his hands and rolled his eyes heavenward. "On this matter, you know that I would like nothing better than to be of help," he said, still not looking directly at Scroop. "It is, as I have pointed out, the fault of the Continental Transportation Code. Beer, cider, distilled spirits and fortified wines may be transported to the distributor authorized in a Closed Environment. Moi! But it says nowhere anything about sacramental wines. Moreover, it is clear, there, that no public or private carrier may transport the intoxicating beverages for an individual in a Closed Environment. Toi! My hands, they are tied," he cried, throwing the said members wide in a rather contradictory gesture.

Scroop clucked to himself in disappointment. "Henri," he reproved, "have you no pride in your own company? A company looking to its three-hundred-and-fiftieth birthday?" Henri looked bewildered at the cleric's seeming shift of subject. Scroop used the tone one normally reserves for scolding children. "The Hudson's Bay Company has always enjoyed certain exemptions from enacted legislation. Always!" he emphasized the last. "The final volume of regulations from the Department of Transport in Old Canada retained most of those exemptions for townsite branches and among them were many that maintained good relations between the Church and the Company. Now the Americanadian Continental Transportation Code says: 'Except where specifically altered in the following document, existing legislation of both countries shall remain in effect.' I can give you the exact passages which allow you to transport sacramental wine for all good Christian purposes." He dropped a sheet of foolscap on Henri's desk, with a single short, scribed line of letters and numbers.

The rotund mayor-manager was clearly stunned. Scroop rose stiffly and began to button his parka, then turned and faced him. "About the child, Henri. It will comfort your soul to know that she was not certifiably dead when *I* reached the dispensary." Then he intoned sternly: " 'It is a stiff-necked people and I will bend them.' You know the verse? I will give you your penance in the proper place." As he stalked from the office Henri stammered, "Good day, Father," and Scroop wondered as he walked down the stairs whether it had been a conscious capitulation.

It was not quite 18:00 and he still had two appointments and he was bone tired. He sat in the autoteria toying with his food, not really hungry and afraid to eat too much lest he get dull. Autoteria food was all the same anyway, he decided, which was only half the truism since all food was literally the same whether you dialled it here or at home. He hadn't really enjoyed eating since Martha's death and no one became a gourmand on a spiritual advisor's credits once his Family AP was gone. Bitter humour, he thought looking at his newer All Purpose Card. At his age and in this place he was suddenly receiving more credits than he had ever dreamed of—for "hardship allowance". Yet this was luxury compared to the conditions in that old ELS, with seven kids and a wife crammed into triple-tiered bunks and his work to clear away before they could eat in shifts.

The gnawing pain was with him again; loss of something more than family. Back then he had known a deep contentment that had nothing to do with material things or close relationships and for a fraction of a second he had glimpsed it again, as he was leaving Henri LeBlanc's office. To serve a spiritual need once more, instead of manipulating the maze. He tossed off the rest of his coffee, slipped his AP Card into a pocket and left his half-finished meal.

All family accommodation in Tundra City was essentially the same, differing only in the number of bedrooms, yet Cyril Jameson and his wife had managed to make their flat look somehow more finished. Not exactly elegant, more like the picture of what an elegant home ought to be. The town engineer-school principal ushered Scroop in with an offhand casualness, graciously offered a drink which was graciously declined and settled his lean, athletic body into a graceful chair. After the required preliminaries, his wife excused herself.

"Now, sir, how can I help you?" Jameson asked expectantly. Scroop, who had already probed without success for a chink in this armour of gentility, decided that there was no longer any virtue in playing by Jameson's rules.

"We could start," he said brusquely, "with my WC."

Jameson's face went a startled blank, and the seconds lengthened until he responded lamely: "I see. Or rather, I'm not sure I do see."

Scroop was relentlessly tactless. "Perhaps I should have said," he continued, "my lack of a WC. You must surely have answered my memo personally, since your name is scribed at the bottom."

Jameson coloured slightly. "Actually," he said, "I did see your memo, but I, uh, turned it over to my clerk. Part-time, you know." Then he seemed to draw up a little more assurance. "Nevertheless, I do recall the answer made very clear our reasons for not providing a — bathroom—in your quarters. For the time being." He managed to look a bit offended. "I would have thought that this was hardly the place . . . "

Scroop cut him off with a guffaw. "Course not," he replied, and sprawled slightly on the divan, obviously not to be budged for some time.

Jameson rose and asked, "Sure you won't have a drink? I think I'll have one myself, after all." He slotted the Family AP and dialled jerkily, then returned to sit and sip with clear apprehension over what gauche act Scroop would commit next. That worthy straightened and looked him in the eyes. "Jameson," he said in businesslike tones, "there have been no confirmations in this parish since it was first opened. Yet there are at least two dozen people of a proper age. Why haven't they been instructed?"

Jameson looked into his glass and answered in a faintly amused tone, "You know yourself that I'm only a lay reader, not a deacon."

Scroop tapped a finger on his knee in annoyance. "Come now," he retorted, "there's been a ruling on that for centuries. In remote parishes a lay reader, or even a warden, may be so empowered. That power has been implicit with your licence from Howard Keewatin." Scroop waved a stiff hand as Jameson angrily leaned forward. "I know, I know. Now it's my job. Classes will be announced next Sunday. Next, I want you to find something appropriate for a baptismal font."

Jameson shot to his feet. "No!" he shouted. "That's too much. No agent of CUSS is going to baptize children in my parish." He flushed and a vein swelled at his temple.

Scroop said quietly, but ominously, "Sit down, Jameson. Your parish? Not yours, or mine. But you are my lay reader, so long as I make the annual request." He waited until the angry man had regained control and understood the threat. "Now," he said, "let me tell you something that none of you has taken the trouble to look up. Henry Danbury presided at my ordination, many years ago. Nevertheless, I took some precautions when I came, including a call when I stopped over at Churchill. The bishop of Keewatin made it to the heliport in time to place his hands on my head and bless me."

Jameson was clearly shaken by the revelation, but he appeared not to be finished. "All right," he conceded, "we'll grant your apostolic succession. We'll grant the UN ruling on our petition, that one CUSS advisor may serve the townsite." He smiled bitterly. "It's too bad you didn't have more time with the bishop. He could have told you why he hasn't sent a priest to us. Why he won't come himself, even if we have a hundred children ready for confirmation."

Suddenly hyper-alert, Scroop couldn't have cared less for the moment who was winning the battle of wills here. This was vital information which he had not been able to unearth. Jameson, in his agitation, hardly noticed Scroop's interest. "Sure, each denomination wanted its own priest, and that seems inefficient. But don't fool yourself that the general manager could have kept them out for long on that ground. Hobbs may be a virulent atheist but he's not an idiot. Our worker priests could have qualified as legitimate personnel even under his interpretations."

Jameson thrust clenched fists into the pockets of his lounging suit, stamped across the room, and swung around scowling. "It's the nature of the beast behind the ridge," he said. "Or its potential nature. Somehow the rumour got around that we were separating radioisotopes. Particularly the stuff used in fission weapons. The worst part of it is that it's possible, theoretically. We have magnetic centrifugal separators at the refinery. The ore is rich in half a dozen heavy metals, including uranium. Put the method and the material in the same place and then try to explain to the average man what the difference is between our 'floaters' and a plasma separator."

Scroop didn't have to be a genius to understand. Jameson could see he was following. "So there isn't a priest in Old Canada," he finished, "who will come to Tundra City, or any sect that will send one. Meanwhile, Hobbs plays it cosy and denies just hard enough to keep the rest of the world relatively convinced that we're not warmongers, including the UN and CUSS."

There was a long silence before Scroop finally spoke. "You said, I believe, theoretically possible?"

Jameson puffed his cheeks in exasperation. "Not you too? Of course it's theoretically possible. Even a civil engineer like me can tell you that. But not with the same equipment. So how do you hide an operation like that?"

Scroop nodded apologetically. "I'll take your word for it." He got up with genuine reluctance and said with less genuine optimism, "I do have two more pleasant things to tell you. First, we should have official sacramental wine for communion when Henri's next shipment comes from the Manitoba Liquor Commission. Second, there's a cassette alongside my scanner which says, 'I will be in Tundra City some time next fall. Howard Keewatin.' He sounds like a man who tends his flock."

It struck Scroop, as he made his way back to City Center, that Jameson would worry over his reaction to the nuclear weapons rumour. Could it be that a CUSS advisor was better than no priest at all? It wouldn't last, though, and the Anglicans, with that infuriating diffidence which seemed inherent, would be the last to accept him. After all, he thought wryly, there was that ancient joke—how did it go?—about God coming home to Old Canada to live with his Anglican heirs. He doubted that the joke would go over well with Alvin Hobbs.

The muted hum of a vehicle brought him back to the present with a slight start, and he moved quickly to the corner of the main intersection to wave down the approaching service truck.

"Goin' through, padre?" the driver asked and Scroop sighed wearily as he folded his long body into the passenger seat. The young man dialled up and they accelerated smoothly towards the tunnel mouth. Shifting a wad of something to his other cheek with a trace of embarrassment, he glanced sideways at Scroop and cleared his throat. "I been meanin' to get to mass regular," he began, "now you're here. Went for a while, but Henri and most of the rest speak French, an' . . . "

He trailed off and Scroop said gently, "I understand, my son. A habit broken is hard to restore." They were into the tunnel now (another way around the Protected Environment regulations), but he ignored the mine entrance and ore cars on the right, the river access branch and storage chambers to the left. With studied casualness he asked, "When was the last time your confession was heard?"

The driver drummed nervous fingers on the steering wheel, then answered, "Before you came." There was awkward silence and he blurted out, "Before I came two years ago."

They came out into grey light and the driver turned hard right with visible relief, dialling off to a quick stop in front of the Admin. Building. Scroop levered himself out on to the foam and leaned back into the cab. "Confession for third-shift RC's is 06:30 Thursday mornings. There's no queue," he added, and stood with bare hand in a half-gesture of benediction while the truck pulled away. He noted with satisfaction that he had three minutes to spare before his appointment with Hobbs, at 21:20.

The office was the man; an extension of Alvin Hobbs's personality. One saw first the massive, tidy desk, then the severe, solid chairs and file decks, after that the unrelieved walls of simulated oak, the deep brown carpet, and finally the panoramic sweep of industrial complex framed by recessed tan curtains. The general manager, veteran of many union and government battles, stood at his window in clear command of the scene: mine, smelters, separators, power plant; the complete site. Scroop knew that he was supposed to be intimidated, aware of how insignificant he and his problem were.

"Then it's no again?" he asked slowly.

"I'll disregard the 'again', Scroop," the manager replied evenly. "Aside from the fact that you have a wide scope for recreation at City Center, I have many reasons for not allowing this silly proposal."

Scroop tried a placatory tone. "Sometimes when you settle into a comfortable routine, you don't realize that you're using the facilities in a monotonous fashion; getting stale."

"Nonsense," Hobbs snapped. "I hardly get over to use them any . . ." He flushed and switched his ground. "Having a number of kids in the complex for a prolonged period is out of the question. Why do you think they put the townsite on the other side of the ridge to begin with? That's a nuclear power plant." He jerked a thumb in the direction of the window.

Scroop caught him up. "But I understand that groups are brought over by Mr. Jameson occasionally, for a half-day lecture."

Hobbs reeled off with relish: "Americanadian Multi-Related Industries Operations Regulations: Section 432; paragraphs 18 to 20. For educational purposes, under supervision, when accompanied by a school official. And your snow sculpture contest doesn't qualify."

Scroop wasn't done yet, however. "Surely the heliport," he persisted, "in a fairly shielded area behind an outcropping, doesn't come under the same regulations?"

Hobbs smiled thinly. "Probably does, at my discretion," he purred, "but in addition, you cannot allow the SAC to be interrupted over a heliport, except during landings and takeoffs. International Closed Environment Standard Legislation: Volume Two: Section SAC; Sub-Section Air Transport; Regulation One. So your budding artists may not collect a foot or so of snow on my heliport and roll it into glorified snowmen." He gestured impatiently as Scroop began yet again.

"And there's no way they will set foot outside the SAC in violation of the World Court Protected Environment Agreement."

Scroop murmured "Ah, yes, we don't need chapter and verse on that. No, what I was going to suggest was that exceptions have been made to the heliport rules. I've seen a very old notice about a kite-flying contest. It couldn't have been held on the Center playing field." He went on more quickly. "The regular flight got away this morning. We've three free days then, there's a nice storm brewing and we could have the port clean and dry, with the sculpturing on one of the spare pads, in forty-eight hours."

Even in mid-sentence, Scroop sensed that Hobbs had been waiting for this. The manager glanced at his chrono and moved towards the door. "I'm busy, Scroop," he said with a patronizing air. "Too busy for people who don't grasp what life up here is all about. Stick to preaching. I suppose you know the rules and regs of that." He opened the door and motioned Scroop through. "Meanwhile," he ended, "I have another appointment. With some officials who just arrived by copter." The barb was flicked with seasoned skill and Scroop knew the timing of their meeting had been nicely calculated.

Equally calculated was the cold dismissal as they moved into the anteroom, where Hobbs nodded curtly and then boomed an effusive, "Welcome to Tundra City, gentlemen," at the two men before his secretary's desk. Unfortunately, there was too little room for Scroop to leave unnoticed and he found himself facing a small, turbanned individual whose black eyes shone like buttons, pulling ancient fabric into a maze of fine wrinkles. Those eyes, without haste, took in Scroop from head to toe, pausing fractionally at the venerable symbol on his breast. Somehow, while returning a soft "Thank you, Mr. Hobbs," he halted Scroop with a slightly raised finger. "An equal pleasure," he added, "to be met by Dr. Scroop."

Hobbs was obviously disconcerted, yet he covered his reaction extremely well. Even so, it seemed to amuse the second man, burly, dark-haired, untidy looking. With only a breath of disbelief in his voice, Hobbs asked, "You've met then?"

The small man smiled serenely and answered, "Not in the flesh, sir. If I may . . . ?" He bowed slightly towards his companion and said formally, "Dr. Scroop—Dr. Horwitz. And I am Rahjan Sikh." He turned back to Hobbs and said pleasantly, "We are here primarily, of course, to discount certain misunderstandings, as technological observors. But you have here a religious anachronism which is peculiarly apt for me and for Jacob, who heads the Semitic League delegation."

Horwitz, who had watched with seeming detachment, stepped forward and extended his hand. "You are the same Scroop then. *Neo-Rational Theology and the Cambridge Platonists.* I read it at New Union Seminary when I took rabbinical orders. Before the metallurgical degrees at home. A long . . . a while back." Scroop winced inwardly despite Horwitz's attempt to gloss the slip.

He was spared an answer when Sikh took up the conversation again. "We three must talk at length, Dr. Scroop. In a way we all operate in a dual capacity, as holy men and technologists and there is much you can tell us about unabsorbed sects in isolated communities, particularly with your specialization." Then with the same effortless capacity he seemed to release Scroop and draw Horwitz and Hobbs into the office. Scroop shook his head at the incredible power of the man — the "Miracle Worker of the Punjab"—and could well believe that he deserved his international reputation. He wondered what Hobbs would make of Sikh's comment about their dual capacities, for it was fairly clear that the manager had not yet recognized why Scroop, of all spiritual advisors, should have been sent here.

He was in luck again: the VIP wagon was still in front of the Admin. Building when he came out and he persuaded the driver that there would be plenty of time to run him under to City Center. He had hardly the time to savour the luxury of the ride when his chauffeur dialled off and he was left standing on aching legs. It seemed a worse indignity than usual to walk the length of the busy gym, pick up his toilet kit and walk half the length back to the men's locker room and showers. Moreover, though the hot water soaked out some of his deep physical fatigue, it served only to release the other, the spiritual pain.

Despite his real need for sleep, when he retired to his quarters he opened his prayer cabinet, rolled out the mat and sank to calloused knees. With eyes on the composited symbol within, he turned his mind to the preliminary disciplined associations. His thoughts swung from the open-bottomed Omega, signifying the dispensing of all things to men, to the over-printed Alpha, narrowing upward to the infinite point of Godhead. Slowly the period of those pendular thoughts closed, focussing on the cross at the centre of the symbol, the cross in which all crosses were captured and Scroop entered the sanctuary of prayer.

He surfaced dizzily out of clinging sleep, to realize that the vidphone had been chiming insistently in the office for some time. Making his groggy way to the scanner desk, he spoke furrily into the phone and squeezed his eyes shut once or twice in an effort to read his chrono dial. It was 05:34 and the voice speaking in his ear said, "Horwitz! Jacob Horwitz. I'm at the dispensary. Sikh had a heart seizure earlier this morning. He managed to call for aid, but by the time the doctor reached him it was too late. I thought you should be the first to know, because it may present complications." Which was probably the prime understatement of Scroop's lifetime.

By 08:00, Scroop was beginning to realize just how many and how far-reaching the complications were. To begin with, he had learned while signing the death certificate at the dispensary that Sikh was not Rahjan's family name, but the generic one given him by adoring compatriots. So far as they were concerned, he was The Sikh, the religious example for a people. Try as he might, he could not seem to make the importance of this clear to an irritable, or more accurately, a hostile Alvin Hobbs. The manager had at first refused to see the spiritual advisor, fobbing him off with a suggestion that he send a memo and it had only been when Scroop threatened to bring Horwitz into it that Hobbs had backed down. He was still, however, boiling at intrusion into his normal schedule.

"Look," said Scroop patiently, "the UN delegation demanded first that the body be taken immediately to the nearest international airport and flown directly to the Punjab."

Hobbs snorted in derision. "With that storm out there it will be three days before we can get the copter out, if we're very lucky."

"I told them that," Scroop explained, "and they said what about a boat to Churchill."

Hobbs clapped a hand to his forehead. "Don't they know anything?" he groaned.

Scroop plodded on. "I told them that the ice is rotten and even a hovercraft wouldn't be safe from sudden upthrusts, but nevertheless a boat couldn't get through."

Hobbs said sarcastically, "Well, at least you've learned something about life up here."

Scroop ignored it, and continued. "So we have the alternatives of preserving the body until it can be removed for burial, which the delegation say can be no more than three days anyway with stretching the laws, or giving it the proper rites here, which involve cremation, preferably on a pyre, and casting the ashes into a river."

Hobbs looked closely at Scroop, disbelief growing visibly. "Those are alternatives?" he asked. "Here?" He collapsed into his chair in a fit of laughter. Then, more soberly, he looked again at Scroop and said, "Come on, now. How can you be serious? And after all, what does it matter to you? Oh I know, he's an international figure, but who besides a bunch of perpetually starving Indians is going to complain if we can't give him a royal send-off?" He smiled nastily. "Anyway, you're a Christian. Why should you muck around with a dirty heathen?"

Scroop felt anger swell his throat shut, choking off any reply. Hold it, he thought, as reason took over, that's a question my new congregations might well ask. But the answer is so fundamental, his mind—or heart—said. So fundamental, indeed, that he was at a loss to put it into words. He gritted his teeth and turned away in disgust, starting to slip his parka over the white utility suit which hung on his gaunt frame. Inexplicably, his silence seemed to goad Hobbs almost beyond control, for he shouted at the back of Scroop's silver-haired head: "Listen! It's your problem. You're so all-loving; you work it out. But I refuse—this office refuses—to be involved."

So it was that a dispirited, dull Scroop, head beginning to throb slightly from tension and fatigue, found himself moving almost dream-like through a day much like the previous one save that yesterday he had been on the offensive. Now he was groping after solutions that he knew didn't exist, possibilities that he knew were at best improbabilities.

First on the list was Henri LeBlanc, whose answers were as predictable as the fact that he resented his recent humility. "It is known to me, all too painfully, that there are only two drawers in the dispensary morgue," he said, pressing a hand to his chest. "Are they not both occupied by members of the True Faith? If Mr. Hobbs had not made certain that the dispatcher was an obstructionist, the body of my poor cousin Claude would be by now in St. Felicien." He sighed gustily. "It would not be taken kindly by us if the dear departed members were in any way disturbed until they are removed from the townsite.

"But," he said with a hint of challenge, "you have the powers, my dear sir. You may not order that they be put together in the one drawer, of course, for that is specific in the regulations."

Scroop tried to concentrate on this potential loophole and drew himself up short, recognizing that Henri was dangling bait. "No, what about the cold rooms and freezers here at the Company?" he asked, and Henri smiled in false sympathy.

"It is again, quite obviously, against the regulations of the public health. I have already prepared the citations for you." He smiled again, dropping a sheet of foolscap into Scroop's lap. "One may not put the body of even a true believer into those places." Scroop did not deny him his moment of triumph; he left while the portly mayor still oozed unctuous sorrow.

Vladmir Homynyk didn't trouble to disguise his delight at the turn of events and he too was totally prepared for and totally unsympathetic to Scroop's problem. The spiritual advisor, a big-city man, had been only dimly aware of that phenomenon of small communities called instant relay. But Homynyk met every query with detailed information, all of it negative, which revealed that he had been preparing almost from the moment of Sikh's death. Scroop had the feeling that he was being moved along a giant maze until he either dropped from exhaustion or gave up.

"Surely," Vladmir stated, "a chaplain of the Union knows that in a mine the temperature increases. And if that weren't enough, you know we fill in the older shafts with the slag. As for the storage chambers along the river access branch, nothing may be placed in them which could attract carnivores." He shook his head as Scroop objected. "Nothing! No matter what it's sealed in. Although it's actually left open to the atmosphere, it's interpreted as part of the Closed Environment. Now the wharves . . . " and he paused until Scroop roused himself to sniff at the carrot. "The wharves," he continued, "are part of the Protected Environment and nothing may be left on them except in the course of loading or unloading cargo." It was rather a crude ploy, if not actually vicious and it stung Scroop sufficiently to make him more alert.

"All right," he admitted, "you can't help me to hold the body until the storm blows over. But isn't there any way to cremate it? The separators are out, naturally, but what about the smelters?"

Vladmir's face reflected first surprise, indicating that he had not considered this, then distaste and finally near-nausea as he all-too-vividly did consider it. "Do you remember what's done to the ore before it's fed through the slots into those smelters?" he swallowed. "Say you were desperate enough to do that to a body. How would you separate the ashes from the slag?"

Scroop nodded mutely and picked up his parka again. He had been going to stop by the autoteria for a late breakfast, but instead he would go straight to the school to talk with Jameson.

"My dear fellow," Jameson said in syrupy tones, "I sympathize with you, but I fail to see how I can help you in any way." A tiny tug at the corner of his mouth belied the tone of voice. "Before you even ask, the refrigeration plant is out. We looked into that last year when Henri got an overshipment of beeves for the catering service."

Scroop brushed the suggestion away with a gesture of annoyance. "Next," he said, "you'll tell me that we can't dispose of the body in the sewage plant, or burn it in the fake fireplace at City Center." He gathered up his energy, uttered a mental prayer, and went on. "What I had in mind was a trifle different. We can't do a proper mortician's job on the body, but it could be placed in a closed container on the rink and allowed to lie in state for a few days. Surely people won't mind giving up their skating for that long."

For a moment Scroop had a wild hope that he'd won, but then Jameson shook his head. "Won't do, y'know," he said. "We looked into that sort of thing too, for an ice fair with booths. Can't put anything like that on the rink. Sinks in, after a while, and could easily cut the piping. The nature of ice, of course. You wouldn't want that gas escaping."

Scroop resisted an insane temptation to drag the engineer from behind his desk and into a classroom, just to see what third manner he would adopt there. He was beaten, however: finished; and as frustration settled crushingly upon him all he wanted to do was go back to his quarters and stretch out.

In the bleak comfort of home, the fact that he had been defeated at his own game somehow hurt much less than that he had failed in a real case of spiritual necessity. He was willing to take a setback as technological expediter, although that had become so much a part of his existence that he had virtually lost his original purpose in mastering the craft. That was the crux of it, wasn't it? Something in him had reawakened—the minister to the spirit—and at the first real challenge he had gone down like a gutted tenement. Dare he question the Supreme Intellect, and ask if the humbling of an old man was worth the repercussions in that troubled international world outside? It was ironic too that the reawakening had been aided by one whose strong spiritual values were alien to Scroop. A lesson for the old man in this as well? But by whatever God one worshipped, Sikh deserved a far better exodus than seemed inevitable. Even Hobbs, the atheist, should see that or be made to see it. Not his problem! "I refuse to be involved!"

Scroop's fingers dug into the edges of his mattress as he stared at the grey-white ceiling, incensed by the callousness of the man. "Refuse to be . . . " But—what if Hobbs were involved? What if it were made his problem? Scroop's pulse quickened. That wasn't quite the solution, but it was a pointer. Stirring at the back of his mind was a very recent memory, together with an older one, much older, of a spider that built on others' webs. With a speed and enthusiasm that threatened bones and tendons, he rolled off the bunk and headed for his scanner, thrusting his classification key into the computer console on his way by. Whatever he might have lost over the years, he had served society and his parish well as a master technologist. Here perhaps the best way to expedite was to allow his victims to spin their own web and even add a little to it.

If Hobbs had been angry yesterday morning, on this successive morning of interruption he was livid. He stood with his feet planted far apart, gazing the length of the table to the four men at the end of the conference room.

"Scroop—Jameson," he sputtered, "if this isn't a bona-fide, first-class emergency; if this has anything to do with that—that stiff over there, I'll have both of you out of Tundra City within the hour! Walking back to Churchill through that blizzard."

Looking innocent but concerned, and far more relaxed than a man with his problem ought to be, Scroop left it to Jameson to answer. The engineer, though obviously uncomfortable, could hardly back down now, after calling the first such meeting in the townsite's brief history. Still he spoke to Hobbs at first with careful deference. "There's a genuine emergency, all right," he began, "and Henri and Vladmir both agreed at once. It was, uh, Reverend Scroop who pointed it out. The fact still remains, whoever discovered it, that we must deal with it immediately, ah, Mr. Hobbs."

Henri LeBlanc and Vladmir Homynyk nodded agreement and muttered a bit, clearly at a loss to suggest any cut-and-dried answer.

To the impatient Hobbs this seemed a further irritant, and he burst out with, "Well, man, can you let me in on it, or am I supposed to wave a magic wand in the general direction of the townsite? What is it that you can't solve among yourselves?" Scroop noted with quiet satisfaction that, far from cowing the trio, Hobbs was bullying them into sullen obstinacy.

Jameson, having begun, seemed delegated to continue, so he squared his shoulders, glanced around at the others and addressed the explosive Hobbs. "It seems that when the tractor train left, the roughnecks forgot to take some stuff back with them. A rather large pile of crating, wooden crating, for hauling the foam layers. It's sitting in sub-division four." He trailed off lamely into silence.

Hobbs stared at Jameson, at all of them and drew a long breath. "There must be more," he said ominously. "You wouldn't bother me just for this."

Jameson went on doggedly. "It really isn't more than that," he replied. "There is a very large pile of combustible material in sub-division four of the townsite. In violation of the International Closed Environ. . .ment Standard Legislation." Hobbs finished.

"Yes, we all know. So? Move it! Why bother me?" Jameson subsided with a feeble laugh and said, "Gentlemen?"

Henri grunted and absent-mindedly scratched his paunch.

"We find it is not so simple as that. To where do we move this, ah, material?" He somehow made the last word sound unsavoury.

Jameson reared up again. "Everyone will agree that it can't be left lying out on my construction site, now that the SAC is meshed. In fact, it can't be left lying out anywhere in the townsite."

Henri stirred himself and added defensively, "Yet it must also be agreed that it cannot be stored on the Company's premises. The regulations, they are very precise on this. In any building, or adjoining annex of any building in which the public is allowed, for business or recreation."

"Or worship," Scroop said mildly, drawing a withering glance from Hobbs.

"Or anything," said Henri. "So any of the buildings in the townsite are unsuitable." Despite himself, Hobbs was beginning to see the intriguing difficulties, but he was in no mood yet to be drawn in.

"Where do you store lubricants?" he asked Jameson, who sounded slightly condescending when he answered, "I doubt any of them would qualify as combustibles these days, but they would be stored in small containers near any machinery that hasn't a lifetime seal."

Hobbs turned to Henri. "How does your liquor get by? And what do they ship it in? How do you dispose of it?"

Henri looked positively petulant. "Perhaps you are thinking of the old-fashioned cardboard?" he asked. "Plastic—a quick-deteriorating plastic. Even the bottles, Mr. Manager. I would be pleased to show you the stockroom, to catch you up on the developments."

The general manager's eyes glinted at the implied insult, but he checked his anger and turned to Vladmir Homynyk, who had remained pensively silent. Now, with Hobbs, Jameson, and LeBlanc all looking at him, he cleared his throat nervously. "I don't have it all here at my fingertips," he said, "but I can tell you pretty straight there's no place I'm in charge of where you're goin' to put that stuff." To Hobbs's flaring anger he said simply, "Listen! I got the safety of my men to consider. Combustibles are deadly in a Closed Environment. Then how you gonna put 'em around the smelters or separators, or in the mine?" He was probably the least devious in the group at this moment, for he turned to Scroop and explained. "I suppose you're thinkin' of the mine like Hobbs thinks of the liquor. Well, we gave up timberin' years ago. It's all fibreglass knock-ups."

Scroop said mildly again, "I noticed, Vladmir."

"Good," retorted the steward. "And you probably remember what I said about the storage areas in the river access branch. Or on the docks. Well, I know without lookin' that what I told you about a body goes double for anything combustible." He gave Henri and Cyril a hard glance and said grimly, "You're not gonna pass that stuff under to us."

What followed was actually nothing more than what had gone before, save that as they took turns using the conference chamber scanner they tangled themselves more thoroughly in red tape, hope sank, and tempers rose. Scroop watched with considerable interest as they became inextricably bound by regulations, while at the far end of the chamber Hobbs exchanged the paleness of anger for the apoplectic hue of an incipient stroke.

"Stop it!" he finally shouted down the table at them. There was a shocked silence, a collective air of shattered dignity and then the trio tried to regain their composure.

Had he been more sympathetic or more constructive, Hobbs might have saved the situation at that point. For once in his long career, however, he made the mistake of speaking to the superficial, when he should have attacked the serious aspect of the problem. Admittedly it was ludicrous to be arguing over a pile of scrap wood, but the man who has been stymied by a two-credit puzzle has ceased to see the humour of his situation.

"You sound like a bunch of school-kids," he told them. "Try behaving like adults, for a change."

"Mr. General Manager," said an icily-proper Henri LeBlanc, "as the so-called mayor of Tundra City, I tell you this. I am going to have that wood shipped to the Admin. Building when I get back and it will be your problem, not ours." Cyril and Vladmir cried in unison, "Hear! Hear!" and Hobbs, hoist by his own petard, smiled sickly at them all and scrabbled mentally after a solution.

"All right," he said, "send it to the heliport and I'll have it looked after."

"You wouldn't be . . . but of course not." Scroop cut himself off, as if what he had been thinking were impossible.

Vladmir caught him up. "Wouldn't what?"

Scroop laughed uneasily. "Oh, for a moment I could see the general manager opening the SAC over the heliport and burning the wood. After all, one can burn organic waste in a Protected Environment, so long as proper safety precautions are taken and the terrain is undamaged. I could probably find the regulations."

From the look on Hobbs's face, that was exactly what he had been considering, but Scroop hurried on. "The general manager has only recently informed me, however, that you cannot allow the SAC to be interrupted over a heliport except during landings and takeoffs. International Closed Environment Standard Legislation: Volume Two: Section SAC . . . "

"Sub-Section Air Transport. Fine, Scroop," Hobbs said dully, "you've made your point. I suppose *you*, having brought the whole matter to our attention, can provide an answer."

"Perhaps I can," Scroop answered, and surprisingly not even Vladmir was surprised, since the painful pattern of the last few hours was suddenly very clear. The spiritual advisor moved to the scanner and dialed. "There is a point at which the Aquatic Pollution Acts and the Protected Environment regulations are in precise agreement. Ah, here, I believe." He slowed the scanner from high to mid-speed, to slow, and froze a frame, almost in one movement. "A community of fewer than ten thousand may deposit directly into a river of, etcetera, cubic metres of flow per minute . . . well above our figure anyway . . . one kilo of organic waste per person per annum, provided it is biologically and chemically inert: for example, treated sewage, organic ash . . . That's what we want, gentlemen."

To the somewhat puzzled trio he explained. "Organic ash! We take the wood out on to the ice and burn it. It will weigh far less than the maximum as ash, won't it, Cyril?"

The engineer nodded almost imperceptibly, then more vigorously as he saw the perverse simplicity of it. "Weight?" he said enthusiastically. "Hardly a factor at all."

Scroop smiled sweetly at him, at all of them. "Fine," he said. "I was hoping you would tell us that. Then I don't suppose there could be any objection if I allow the dispensary the use of its whirlpool bath again? The staff have been terribly patient, but they do need it."

More puzzled than ever, the trio looked as if they thought he had cracked under the strain. "Allow me, Scroop," Hobbs called from the far end of the room. "What our good spiritual advisor means is, why not put a body on top of the pile?" He walked to stand directly in front of Scroop. "I personally can find no objection here and now. Can you?" he addressed the other three. "If you can, of course, I'm willing to bet that Dr. Scroop has found a loophole."

There was naked hatred in his eyes as he turned again to Scroop. "I think we will all have learned something from this exercise," he said. "For that reason it is valuable. You evidently regard the disposal of Sikh's body as of sufficient importance to jeopardize your future here. Make no mistake. Until this morning I was willing to tolerate your presence." He glanced around at the others. "You may be able to understand his motives better than I," he snarled, and left the conference chamber.

That was a question to ponder, Scroop thought, as he straightened with the body of Rahjan Sikh on his shoulder. Behind him, as he moved stiffly down the dock ladder and carefully out on to the rotten ice, there were a large number of his charges watching. Ahead, Jacob Horwitz was putting the last piece of wood on the pyre and he came back to help Scroop carry Sikh the rest of the way. In defiance of the stinging snow, the whipping tail-lash of the blizzard, he had his parka hood thrown back, and on his head sat a mitre with golden embroidered words—*Kadosh ladonai.* Scroop had not realized how great was this man's religious stature too. Beneath their feet the ice groaned and heaved and as soon as the body was safely placed the spiritual advisor insisted that his helper return to safety. It was as dark as it would get at this time of year, helped by the storm. Nowhere near as dark as the ignorance of man. And one loves men *for* their faults, not despite them, Scroop recalled, with a flood of compassion for those who watched. He didn't know if a single one of them understood why he was doing this. Cooking oil doesn't burn all that hot, but Scroop had obtained a fair amount from the catering centre.

Enough to get the crating burning at the base.

He pulled a sheet of foolscap from his parka pocket, and began reading a completely unfamiliar ceremony by the fire's light, a cere-mony so old that it might not be in present use in the Punjab. It ought to be satisfactory, he decided, as flames shot fifty feet into the air, crackling and throwing an angled spiral three times that length into the fine snow. Through the dancing heat waves he saw the body writhe practically into an upright sitting position as it was enveloped and consumed. Then with a quiet, almost anti-climactic lurch, the ice beneath the pyre opened and what remained slid hissing into the river water. Cracks sprang outward in a crazy web and water washed all the way to Scroop's boots. He turned and groped his way towards the dock, eyes still filled by a great black spiral of flame. *Requiescat in pace,* he added without apology to the ceremony just completed and without hesitation began to whisper the Lord's Prayer. As he mounted the ladder and moved through the crowd, his flock, he intoned *Si iniquitates* and *De Profundis* and it surely was not his imagination when other voices than his closed with *Requiem aeternam.* He swung into the access branch tunnel and two steps to the rear, one to the right, he sensed rather than saw Jacob Horwitz keep pace. It was appropriate, all of it, for in this transitory moment Benjamin Scroop could walk without self-deception, leaving all webs behind him.

B B B

ed cted n
ent ment I

3

Protected Environment

3

When the intercom buzzed he was about five lines from the end of a sheet. He continued methodically removing parts from their containers, making his visual check, replacing them and ticking them off, until he reached the bottom of the sheet. Then he acknowledged the call, carefully placing his clipboard at the stack where he had stopped. On the way by the pumproom he heard the Engineer and the Electrician chatting cheerfully while they worked over standby equipment, but he kept moving in his stolid, purposeful manner, up the ladder to the top deck and left into the control area. The Supervisor turned and crooked a finger, waving him into the dimly-lit section where the display was spread in a gentle curve. "Look," he said. "The 20-30 panel. About 26.4."

The Roughneck had spent all of his adult life working the Pipe, from late teens to his present late forties, and he had coped with each new development as something to be understood and digested so far as it was necessary to his job. Side-angle infrared had been installed for five or six years now, and he had learned to interpret the ghostly "maps" as symbols of his own rich knowledge of the land. Down the middle of each of the ten panels, served by five towers each side of the station, stretched the thin, faint-white length of the Pipe itself— kilometers 1150 to 1250 of the tube that carried Keele River crude south to Dawson Creek and further, to Alberta refineries. On the 20-30 panel he could see, even before the Supervisor centered the zoom screen over it, a white blotch growing canker-like on the Pipe.

The Supervisor motioned to the bank of dials beneath the display. "No pressure loss so there's no leak, but it's coming into the station about two degrees below normal. I read it as at least a bad insulation crack." The Roughneck grunted non-commitally. "Well, likely it is more than that," the Supervisor went on, interpreting the Roughneck's meaning. "Never seen anything like it, though. Happened a little earlier this morning, between 08:15 and 08:30. I've been watching since then." The Roughneck pointed off to the east on the panel, sliding the zoom screen over and down, past the light grey of tree stands and the tiny glints of furred and feathered creatures. "Caribou," he noted. The Supervisor frowned, not sure of what this meant. "Pretty far into the hills," the Roughneck added. "Wolves." He maneuvered the screen into the extreme southeast corner. The Supervisor squinted and shrugged. "I did read the caribou," he said defensively. "I'll bet you can tell a mouse from a midge." The faint sarcasm was lost on the Roughneck, as he swung the screen again, and turned it to full power. "Now this," he pointed, "is new."

It was animal and it was big, and again the Supervisor was faced by a puzzle. Rubbing his blue-black jaw pensively, the Roughneck cocked his head, then concluded, "Bear. Might be the whole answer. They get strange about man stuff." The Supervisor looked very closely: he learned as much as he could when he could. "First one I've seen here," he said. "He's way off the normal range. From the heat he's throwing he's no black. But a grizzly?" The Roughneck grunted again, which this time could mean no.

"At any rate," the Supervisor leaned back in his chair, "you'd better take a look. I don't like sending you now, with a bad one coming in this evening. Late report gives us about eight hours till it gets really rough. With about an hour-and-a-half return, you can't scratch forty minutes at the site." The Roughneck nodded, calculating it doubled and redoubled, and coming up a little short. He moved over to the universal scanner, dialled weather information, ran the satellite stills and read the progs for himself. Then he shrugged and turned to go. "I'll look," he threw back. "Won't take long to stick on a slab of foam."

Down at the lockers he put on his suit, checking it for rips or fraying, running fingers under the nap at collar and cuffs. Carrying headsock, helmet and visor under one arm, gauntlets in the other hand, he walked solidly but not heavily to the garage. Stepping past the long, sleek line cruiser to the small prowler, he checked it from stem to stern with the same care, although he had given it a maintenance tune-up the afternoon before, and then finished dressing. He opened the garage doors, climbed in, and dialled the prowler up a notch feeling the powerful throb right through his boots. All readings were top-gage as he moved out and turned parallel to the Pipe, dialling off a few yards up the track of packed snow. He tried his suit heaters and triggered his radio, then plugged into the prowler's great powerpack and did it all again. The Supervisor acknowledged each time, and he noticed that one of the others had closed the doors. Everything on his mental list ticked off, he slid the canopy closed and flipped to auto, dialling up to 40 kph. Locking in twenty meters from the Pipe, the prowler accelerated smoothly. Satisfied, he flipped to override, his own cautious choice rather than manual, and took the wheel. Outside temperature showed thirty below (Fahrenheit—he'd never got used to Celsius), and a freshening northwest whipped fine snow up across the rounded nose of the prowler. To the east, now closing now receding, a belt of scrub provided all there was of a horizon in the greyish-white of a fleeting winter day.

To those possessed of more imagination, the eastern slope of the Rockies might be visualized as a great, gradual rise, but the Roughneck had known these undulating foothills almost from birth. Now, as he settled back into the padded seat, he chewed over the details of the situation. Grizzly? No. Not this far northeast. Yet it couldn't be a black. Might be a freak cinnamon. Probably some kink in the equipment. Animals were more dependable than man stuff, or men for that matter. Over the years he had evolved a concept of nature which involved a rough kind of predictability. Man was the outsider in this picture, but so long as he tried to fit in he would likely be tolerated. Let him try to change things, however, and sooner or later he would be dealt with. He had a vague impression of some great white beast, set loose by whatever God there was, to flick a paw at this solitary individual or perhaps to tear a settlement to fragments. It was like men to get cocky over their fancy equipment, thinking they were in control of everything. Well, more than one had learned different out in space, with stuff a lot fancier than what he was using. He'd had two flicks in the past himself, for that matter, to keep him in line, and he accepted fatalistically that he was never out of reach. He scowled off toward the west, where the white beast was on the prowl again today, slipping down the fringes of the mountain range.

Thought for the Roughneck was a slow but fairly uncomplicated process, with very little digression and even less backtracking. Consequently, he reached his conclusion about the thing some people call fate just as his speaker crackled, and the Supervisor said: "P32: Station 9. You're there." He thumbed his mike switch once and dialled off to a quick stop, slid the canopy open and had a good long look about through the shifting haze of lifted surface snow. Unplugging, he climbed out and closed the canopy. The Pipe looked too bulky to be resting on the spindly, widely-spaced supports which were all the Protected Environment regulations allowed, but he knew they were far stronger than they appeared, and well-bedded whether they dropped far into muskeg or struck short into solid rock. The only place where the Pipe went under was at major wildlife crossings, and there it must go under by law. Man would protect nature from men, with a loose but lengthy net of regulations stretching all the way to the seats of government. Later in the winter it would be deep in snow anyway, but now the Roughneck was still able to duck beneath and scan the west side of the Pipe. He had overrun the damage site by about thirty meters, but it was bad enough to be seen much further than that. He whistled tunelessly through his teeth as he came down to it and saw that a full meter of Schlagge insulation had been torn away in uneven chunks. Where the tough plastic piping had been laid bare, deep, long score marks glittered moistly at him. Bear it was, a huge one by the distance between claws, and he wished uneasily that the wind hadn't already wiped away all tracks.

As if in answer to his unvoiced question, the Supervisor chose that moment to call. "Your big friend was moving south, ranging on and off the Pipe, but he's found the crossing at '25 and struck off almost due east now. Very erratic. Like a drunk on a flatbed robofreight." It built into a vivid picture for the literal-minded Roughneck as he got about the business of patching. At the prowler he lifted the rear cover and took three pieces of foam, together with a trimmer and liquid bond. The dash chrono showed 11:04, and even with his meticulous care in cutting and fitting the thirty-by-thirty squares he would have ample time to finish. Hands working more or less mechanically in their thin gauntlets, he considered the actions of the animal. Bears could seem to be travelling aimlessly, but still there was a pattern which the Supervisor would have caught by now. If he said erratic he meant it, and there was definitely something abnormal about this bear. He was not unhappy that the animal was moving away. With the wind picking up, the first whirls of falling snow merging into the surface curtain, and visibility drawing in perceptibly, there was enough to keep him busy.

The liquid bond froze a bit as usual, belying its wonder specs, but there was a complete bead which ought to hold until better weather. He cleaned up the site quickly but without haste, knowing that some hard-headed government inspector would complain over anything bigger than a crumb violating the regulations, and returned to the prowler. The way the weather was closing, he might yet have to lock in on auto, but he left trusting to the equipment as a last resort. As soon as he had plugged in and strapped down, he called the station. The Supervisor sounded only slightly relieved as he acknowledged, and it was a mere moment when he called again. "The bear has turned back. Guess he doesn't want to tangle with those wolves. Heading straight for the Pipe. If you move out now you should get by, unless you want to say hello." The Roughneck sent back a curt "Thanks," swung the cat around, and dialled up to 30 kph. Too much, he cursed mildly, having known before he tried that with a wind angling into its tail the prowler got very touchy. He dialled down slowly, testing, until he found reasonable stability at 20 kph, and felt a hint of longing for the simple, rugged vehicles of his youth. For one thing, the racket they made kept lots of distance between him and anything big.

The bear would be heading for the crossing, likely working the ridge above the wide cut that ambled southeast from the Pipe. He'd travelled that area more times than he could count, most of them illegal, and it was an open secret among the flit jockeys who spotted him that the Roughneck could show a man a pleasant tour if he was held over at Station 9. Good country. He could lay it out in his mind, even though the snow and wind had cut visibility to less than twenty-five meters. He stubbornly resisted switching to auto until he was past the crossing and moving up the rise just to the south, noting that the Pipe was blotted out on his right. The prowler was bucking again, trying to keep its tail dry, and he was glad to be by the bear's probable goal. Then, to contradict him, the Supervisor's voice came crackling in, hard and clipped. "He's picking up speed . . . coming in on your south-east. God, he must be moving now. Goose it! Closing like a jet." The Roughneck tried to push his prowler a bit and only slewed half off the trail. He wrestled it back and held steady with jerking muscles, then threw a glance off to his left just as the Supervisor yelled, "Comin' right at you," and had a frozen, sharply-detailed glimpse of the great brown shape hurtling down on him before they met with a wrench-ing, sickening thunk of flesh and metal.

The rear end of the prowler whipped into the air, went over the animal as the machine pivoted on its nose, and came back down with a crunching jar. The hood, punched into a grotesque vee, tore half off the chassis and flapped loosely. Inside the cab, seatbottom ripped clear of flooring and the Roughneck was thrown up against the canopy and dash, to come smashing down across the edge of the tipped seatback. He lay arched over it, a searing bar of paralyzing pain bridging his back, mouth open in a soundless scream, bulging eyes staring up into the whipping snow. Gradually he became aware of the other circle of pain where his helmet had been driven down onto his collarbones. He tried to move and pain blossomed in the small of his back and shot tendrils up his torso, all the way into his arms and head. Horrifyingly, the rest of his body was numb, as if it had gone to sleep. All he was able to manage was a slow, cruelly painful pushing with his elbows, to scrape the seatback along his body and into an upright position. As it reached his shoulders the rest of his body sagged back down, and he realized that the seatbottom was still securely belted to him, though he hadn't felt the weight of it. Hanging on the edge of consciousness, he forced his eyes to focus on the scene outside.

The bear had been lying in a shapeless heap next to the machine, but now it stirred, rolled, and raised its head. The Roughneck could see clearly where, in place of an eye, there was a filthy, matted wound on the right side of the head, white bone showing around the whole back half of the socket. Incredibly, he felt a surge of compassion as he saw that it was old, perhaps weeks old, and knew with appalling certainty that this was the reason for the beast's strange actions. He also saw, with the cold finality that accompanies knowledge of one's errors, that it was a grizzly. The bear seemed completely unaware of him; totally concerned with the prowler. After several attempts it reared up on hindquarters, towering over the vehicle, revealing a terribly crushed right forequarter. Swinging its body from side to side, it reached out a huge left paw and raked claws through the prowler's exposed innards, tearing out power cable and smaller wiring like a ball of spaghetti. It slapped down again, and the hood prop tore loose and clanged across the powerpack, welding itself to terminals in a fountain of blue sparks that sent the bear reeling backward. It staggered off on three legs, leaving a trail of blood, and the Roughneck knew it was done for. Nothing could survive after being stove in like that, and again he felt a surge of compassion as the animal disappeared into the thickening river of driven snow.

A last paradoxical fact suddenly thrust into his mind as he recalled that the bear's hindquarters had been smeared with bright red paint. Park rogue! Men had taken him from where he had been twisted by man's intrusion, and humanely shipped him a thousand kilometers to a protected place where he and men would not meet again. It left maybe a hundred kilometers unaccounted for, but with that background, and that injury, a crazed grizzly could do anything. With his usual lack of bitterness, he swallowed the fact that he'd made a bad mistake, the worst mistake that one could make in his way of life. Someone better at words than he was had said: Plan for the improbable—never rule out the impossible.

Fumbling across his chest with awkward fingers, he triggered the radio once, twice, until it penetrated that the speaker had been long silent. He was regaining control of his upper body, but as he pulled himself toward the dash it felt as if that part of him were set atop some unsteady column of air. Clumsily he unplugged and heard the instant, light crackle as his suitpack took over. The Supervisor was calling insistently, and he triggered again at the first break. He still had his voice, although it went breathy and faded on him after short phrases, and he gave grudging thanks for the little radio that was really designed to carry only to the prowler's booster. The Supervisor obviously got most of what he sent, and filled in the rest from what he'd watched on the panel. "We'll send up the cruiser," he promised, and the Roughneck rested a moment while he listened to Station 10 advise that it had gone on emergency standby. Then, gathering up his strength, he unbuckled, reached up and hauled the crazed canopy open, and levered himself over the side. Headfirst, useless legs flopping, he went down onto the snow, landing heavily on his shoulders and blacking out from the explosion of pain that ripped through his body. He lay sprawled for a long time until consciousness returned, until he had clear vision again and the agony had subsided. Then he dragged himself to the nose of the prowler and sought handholds to pull himself up onto knees that weren't there.

Frost began to build on the edges of the cloth around his nose and mouth, and at the back of his mind he reckoned the temperature had fallen at least ten degrees. That and the wind chill factor made him appreciate the suit and its makers; the ones who had adapted it from space. The wind made a steady moan over the back of his helmet as he leaned in on his forearms and took stock of the damage. That marvel of engineering, the powerpack, was shorted across two segments, and he doubted if there was much left of the third even if the internal relay had kicked out. Nevertheless, he dropped flat again, clenched his teeth and rode out the waves of nausea that rolled through him, and crawled laboriously to the rear of the prowler to haul out tools. Back at the nose he lay sheltered as much as possible and worked the plug off his suit cord, deliberately shutting out the pain which had settled to a steady, taut throb radiating from part way up his spine. He drew a long, fiery cold breath and dragged himself up again to wrap the bared wires around the third segment terminals of the powerpack. Knowing that he might simply be draining his suitpack, he unplugged that and waited for five minutes. By then he was a bit chillier, and he found it hard to hear the speaker, but it seemed to be holding steady, so he slid down to wait, content to bleed whatever was left in the powerpack rather than use the limited supply of the suitpack. The cruiser should be coming in good time.

The Engineer had taken the cruiser after a perfunctory check, locking on while he finished suiting up. He had a great deal more faith in his equipment, and far less intimate knowledge of the world outside, factors which perhaps had some close relationship. It was impossible to use the air cushion under these conditions, and though the cruiser was heavy and relatively unaffected by the wind, its treads actually developed less traction than the prowler's in the dry snow that built high before it. He began bucking drifts, cresting them over the windscreen, and realized that he would have to stay at low dial to get enough bite. His speed was a frustrating 15 kph, and the awesome powerpack of the sleek machine put an ominously heavy strain on its gear train. He was just under twenty kilometers out, ninety-two minutes by the chrono after the Roughneck had called in, when a treadlink sheared, and the load release threatened to tear the craft apart. It was as simple a failure as that, and it brought the multi-thousand credit vehicle, miracle of craftsmanship, to a shuddering, slewing halt.

The Engineer's quick outside examination showed beyond doubt that while he had the parts and tools to make repairs there was no way he would manage it alone in these conditions. Back inside the cabin where he could remain in comfort for a week, if necessary, he called in to the Supervisor and then paced and repaced the short length of the shop bay in a slow rhythm of futility. Over and over in his mind he turned the question of why his precious machinery had failed, managing in this fashion to shut out the soul-destroying question of what would become of the Roughneck.

The Roughneck had no such sophisticated defenses, but then he had long ago come to terms with the ultimate possibility of his job. Just as he had cut his body activity to a minimum, he cut his mental activity, and the past hour or so had ticked by without rousing in him much more than a slight itch of impatience. Suit temperature had fallen to a bare tolerance level, and when he heard the whisper of voices from the speaker he reluctantly pulled the cord loose from the powerpack and replugged his suitpack. Immediately the volume jumped, and he listened to the Engineer's terse report, the Supervisor's response, and seconds later Station 10 flatly stating before the request that its cruiser was on the way with two men aboard. Welcoming the heat that seeped back into his suit, but chafing because it couldn't be lowered and conserved, the Roughneck considered the seventy-five or eighty kilometers between himself and his would-be rescuers. With full use of his legs, it would have worked, even in the storm that was beginning to stalk him.

Rolling onto his stomach, he crawled to the rear of the prowler again, extracted the survival kit, and hung it around his neck, cursing the bulk of it that splayed his arms so wide. Slowly, willing back the pain that flamed through his back and shoulders, he inched his way toward the forbidden belt of scrub, stopping within a few meters of it to pick out a good shelter. It was only after entering the stand, however, that he could see anything through the blinding, driving snow, and he realized with a dull resignation that here was no fir or spruce, with protective skirts to conserve heat. Sheer exhaustion forced him to choose a tiny clearing in the mass of thin alders, and he dropped the kit and lay against it for a good ten minutes before he could collect enough energy to crawl after deadwood. He had no idea of what condition his feet were in: fingers were definitely stiffening, and he wondered idly as he had many times before why gauntlets and boots never seemed as well designed as the rest of an outfit.

When he had brought in everything usable within his limited circuit, he opened the kit and spread his firesheet. Within minutes he had a decent fire going, and went about the business of erecting a low shelter-half. It was virtually impossible to swing a hatchet, a problem which hadn't occurred to him. There seemed no way to place himself on the there-not-there foundation of his trunk so that he wouldn't fall over with every swing. The numbness seemed to be moving up as well, maybe only a trick of fatigue, and he finally gave up and tried to hitch the sleeping bag up his limp legs, past his hips, and around his shoulders. It was more than difficult: it was impossible. Overhead the wind was lacing snow into the treetops with a frightening howl, and he knew that he must soon build a screen for the fire or it would be doused by the maelstrom of snow that swirled over the edges of the clearing. First, however, he must rest and unplug his suit heater.

The Supervisor had followed his progress on the panel with instant understanding, and when the faint patch had been engulfed by a beautiful, swelling blot, he leaned back and wiped beads of perspiration from his face. Nevertheless, he knew too well that if the Roughneck was at all handicapped his chances were slim. Outside temperature was still falling, below fifty now, and the full force of the blizzard hadn't hit them yet. At 14:00 the cruiser had reported severe drifting, and a speed of only 12 kph. A mere twenty kilometers, and sixty more to go, if they made it at all. He sat upright again and stared at the panel, as if he could will heat into the uneven white spot.

The Roughneck had finally stirred and done his best to chop green boughs and make a screen, but he couldn't reach high enough to keep it out of harm's way. Even his pitifully small fire, fed on green stock now, was enough to threaten it, and when he jerkily pushed a new branch in, it scattered the half-burnt pieces. As he watched helplessly, the remaining fire sizzled fitfully against a relentless blanket of thick, wet snow, and the Roughneck knew that his struggle to keep it going was futile. Within half an hour he lay in near darkness, waiting for the time when he must plug in his suit heater again, not sure that he could judge it right when only his upper torso could tell him of its need. The crusted ice around his mouth and nose was nearly closed over when he forced a sticklike finger to pry it away, and palmed the plug back into his suitpack. He had less than two hours, more likely one.

After a while, it became almost pleasant to lie half inside the sleeping bag and let his mind move quietly, steadily among the waking dreams which he had developed and held to across the years. He had always wanted to go to the queen megalopolis, Montreal . . . had a CommChamb pamphlet in his locker, well-worn now, through which he had built his own picture of what it would be like. And once he had even gotten as far as Edmonton before he found, for some strange reason, that he couldn't seem to function properly. Here, in this time of settling stillness, he was finally freed to move where he pleased, and his mind slowly filled with the magnificent colour and sound of the autobars, the wraparound theatres, the scent of big, warm women. This was living.

The Supervisor saw the cruiser creep into panel 40-50, an almost imperceptible movement telling more than words. He had watched the larger spot on the 20-30 shrink in the zoom screen, grow dim, and die, leaving only the faint glow of animal heat. That too had dimmed, until the Electrician reached across his shoulder and adjusted brightness and contrast to the last fraction. Arms rigid, fingers digging into the chair, he strained forward and stared mutely until the spot became a mere illusion of the eye on the panel of the technologist's box, and even that disappeared back into the grey-black pattern of a northern terrain, dusted with its many vivid pinpricks of life.

4

Cain[n]

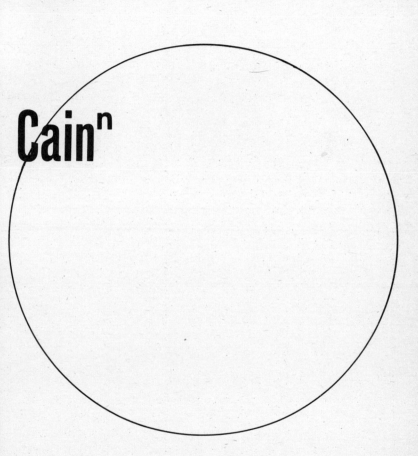

4

. . . and he builded a city.

Genesis 5:16

●

He was poised in a taut half-crouch, ten feet into the great, stark hall, eyes shifting warily from the robocop at the double doors to the young man in the black utility suit. Lip curled in a snarl, black hair wildly tangled, he looked like a savage predator strayed down from the fringes of the Arctic tundra and brought to bay in this keep of civilized man. The golden eyes suddenly glazed as he hissed an obscenity and launched himself at the figure in black, only to crumple in mid-air, as if struck by an invisible bolt. He slid on his back to the young man's feet, arms and legs splayed without control, gazing upward, upward, at the unfocussed face far above him. Slowly strength returned, he saw clearly, and the young man gently reached down and lifted him to his feet. "Peace," he said. "Peace and unity within these walls, and within ourselves."

The robocop moved forward, paused almost imperceptibly as it shifted from programme to central control, and spoke. "Jason Berkley, TOR2712 ONT37643, no AP Card at apprehension. Updated and re-cycled duplicate from Missing Persons is now in your file. Charge, a 291. Apprehended 13:25 Central Daylight; tried 14:30 Toronto General Court. Delivered into your custody 21:10 Mountain Standard." The double doors moved smoothly open as the robocop left, then closed with a solid chunk which belied their simple elegance. The two stood alone, seconds lengthening as they looked one another over carefully, the boy with intense hostility and the young man with haunted compassion. "Jason Berkley," he murmured. "Jason, I'm Orest Lenchuk, and this is Diamond Willow School. We'll be together for a long time, so you might as well learn to get along with me."

Jason made a vicious chopping gesture and turned towards the door, but stiffened as Orest barked, "Don't be stupid! There's no way out of here but acceptance. Turn around!" The boy glared over his shoulder, and Orest went on in a more reasonable tone. "Roll up your right sleeve," he directed, "before you try anything that can get you in trouble." Jason turned back reluctantly and looked down, noting with surprise that he was wearing a grey utility suit. He unsnapped the cuff, pushed the sleeve up jerkily and gasped as a bright metal oval flashed in the diffuse light. He saw with horror that the metal was embedded in his flesh. Even as he watched the surface seemed to shimmer, and a word appeared beneath. Lips moving, he spelled it out. *Dependence.* With uncomprehending shock, he pulled his eyes from the terrible object and gazed at Orest, questioning without words.

Deliberately matter-of-fact, Orest explained. "Takes the Stab about two hours to plant it. Then wherever you are, they can find you. Get close to any restricted area, any tronlock like the ones on all the doors here, they know. They can freeze you anywhere—you've felt it! Until they change it, you live with me and do what I say. We share the same room, go everywhere together, even share a dual AP Card. Only difference is, I can eat on it alone—you can't. You get nothing without me. I teach you. How to get along, to behave. I even run your RehabEd programme. You depend on me. Dependence! Get it?" He paused to let it sink in, then finished. "Come on, let's go to the Stab and get you briefed." Firmly, but not roughly, he placed a hand on the boy's bony shoulder, and steered him towards a smaller door at the side of the hall.

Still bewildered and belligerent, Jason moved into the indoctrination chamber. He slouched uneasily before a TriVid cubicle, trying desperately to remember how he had got here, what had happened earlier in the day, but barely able to picture the robocruiser that had dropped him here. Then the cubicle sprang to life, revealing three stern men facing him. Confused as he was, Jason was alert enough to catch slight differences in the background. The three were in different places. He knew too that this was the first time he'd actually seen TriVid. The oldest, on his left, fixed him with a cold, probing stare from under bushy brows and began.

"Jason Berkley, Americanadian, vagrant, fifteen. You have been charged, tried and found guilty of a capital offence, committed in the megalopolis of Toronto. Because you are three years under statute you have been given into our custody, pending sentence. Because you have been assessed as rehabitable and potentially productive, we have accepted you. Had you been genetically criminal you would have been permanently isolated. Had you been low productive you would have received permanent memory erasure and been retrained for base labour. Despite your previous environment, however, you have high potential and your case contains extenuating circumstances. You will be punished, nevertheless. The law is exact and impartial."

The centre man continued. "You have been brought half-way across the continent to this school in Alberta, with the memory of your crime and any events related to it under block. There will be no perceptible amount of brain damage. We will attempt to develop your social adaptability and intellectual potential to the fullest, in order to utilize your productivity. Society is practical."

There was silence while Jason tried to understand what had been said. A few words were too big, but he was beginning to grasp his situation. Then the last man, on the right, spoke in a soft but powerful voice. "Jason Berkley, we have vested our custody in Orest Lenchuk, your guardian and teacher. He will administer examinations to assess your previous education and to decide where your talents may best be exercised, for society and yourself. Justice tempers the law and guards the individual from society's exploitation. Until you yourself deny it, justice is humane. You may now proceed to Phase One."

Suddenly the cubicle was empty. Jason shook his head and looked frantically for a way out, but there was only the one door and Orest, big and cautious, stood waiting. With the cold, sure knowledge of the trapped animal, he drew into himself as he was led from the room and down the great hall. Orest was talking as he took the boy into a wide corridor lined with doors. Jason half listened while he tried to piece it all together and some essential core of his being waited for the place, the second, of escape. Labs and group rooms, Orest was explaining, and then they were out into the open. His breath caught as Jason saw overhead a sweeping, unbelievable multitude of stars through a transparent roof. Even crouched on a rooftop he had never seen anything like this. Not even a faint haze of smog between him and this vast, overwhelming sight. He shuddered, more and more aware of how pitifully small and alone he was, shrunk to nothing as he looked into infinity.

Then they were back inside and he saw that they had crossed a walkway, only there was no moving belt. And before he could think about that they had entered an autoteria, or something like what he had glimpsed at times, huddled on the servo side. Here there were long tables, and incredibly the place was empty. Sweet pickings, he thought, and then remembered that he was on this side of the serving windows. His first impulse was to grab a chair and shove its legs through the little doors, as his stomach convulsed at the sight of food. But Orest was already moving to them, All Purpose Card in his hand, asking what he would like. Sheer instinct kept him from gorging, and he chose steak, potatoes, rich cake and coffee—more than enough to satisfy but not enough to cut his speed. Even as he ate, he took in every inch of the autoteria with quick, furtive glances, seeking, probing, storing for future reference. Knife and fork were clumsy; he hadn't often used them before, except when he swapped pickings for food with Crazy Almann.

When Jason had swallowed his last, noisy gulp of coffee and wiped greasy fingers on his tunic, Orest straightened from his patient slouch and rose. "Time to sack," he grunted, and more sharply, as Jason pushed back his chair and stepped away, "The dishes go on that belt by the door." For an instant Jason tensed, then shrugged and moved back to put his things on a tray. "Mine too," Orest added, and the boy bit his lip to keep from replying, storing this away too for the future. Together they moved into another corridor, across a dimly lit room with heavy furniture, a thick rug, scattering of wall pictures and shaped objects, and cabinets of real books. His fingers itched as Jason thought of what those would bring in swaps from the Syndies, but they were climbing a flight of stairs. Yet another corridor, a stop in a large common bathroom, and they were in front of an open door. "This is it," Orest sighed, and drew him in to stand gaping. Behind them the door slid silently shut and there was a faint buzz and click. Instantly Jason was there, palming the lock, fingers running up and down the frame. He finally slumped back and turned to Orest, panic barely under control. "Not until 06:00, Jason," Orest said gently. "Not until breakfast. Now why don't you relax and get some sleep?"

The room was smaller than it looked, with closet, bunk and desk lining opposite sides and two lounging chairs and a small table in front of a large window. The drawers in one desk and under one bunk were open and a pile of clothing and blankets was on the desk seat. Orest had already unzipped his utility suit and was slipping into a sleepsuit. He waved an arm at the pile and smiled. "Two of everything you need. One change a day; wash your own. Show you the launderit tomorrow. Keep your side neat and clean. Get your sleepsuit on, make your bed and flake." He slipped into his bunk, flipped open a small head panel and thumbed a switch. His side of the room went black, as if a wall had cut one third from the whole. Jason, crushed by fatigue now, snapped a blanket from the pile, wrapped it carelessly around him and huddled into a corner of the bunk. With leaden fingers he pried open his panel, stared at a row of switches and pushed the yellow one set off by itself. There was nothing but a faint shimmer of light from floor to ceiling, down the centre of the room, and he lay in the dark, mind nearly numb. Finally he gave up to the tremendous need for rest. Restlessly, fitfully, he backed into sleep, until only that extra sense of the hunted remained alert.

There was something behind him, following at a distance: he could sense it without seeing or hearing, and he quickened his pace to the access hatch of the robofreight track. As he cracked the hatch he saw that he was in luck, that a truck was shunting off the main line. The pick-up caught its undercarriage and it moved towards him, rubber wheels whispering. Deftly he swung up over the end rail, balanced and pushed out flat on a packing crate. The truck moved steadily past two block sidings, past the third hatch where Jason would normally have dropped off, past the third siding, and he slipped easily to the side at the fourth hatch. Far down the gloomy tunnel he saw another truck shunt in and—was it?—he knew a figure flitted from the hatch he had used. The muscles across his chest tightened slightly and he felt the quickening, the sharpening that always came with pursuit. Ducking out the hatch, he raced down the narrow corridor, doubling twice through cross-passages and finally knelt above a grill, prying carefully at two corner screws. The square lifted and he slid under, to land crouching on a junction cube in a service tunnel. Cautiously he lowered the grill, making sure the screws fell into place, then flipped down on to the curved conduit and ran again. He threw himself up and across several cubes until, at last, he squirmed off one at right angles and crawled, straddling the smaller conduit, to the end where the distribution panel stood; a bank of seven-foot boxes stretching to either side. He stood up and moved to the last one, fishing in his tattered coverall for a strip of plastic which he slipped behind the catch. The door sprang ajar and he stepped into the empty box and closed it after him. Then he waited.

Unmoving as a figurine, breath slowing to nearly nothing, he waited. Time spun out and he was able to think, though still aware of a questing presence somewhere outside. What had he been doing? He had made a real pick from the storeroom under the autoteria on the thirty-eighth level, used the elevator just like a Mark, got off at sub-three and used the watermain ladder to sub-five. He'd stowed some in his own hole behind the loose panel over the block heater units and taken the rest to Almann. It was vivid now but jumbled, somehow disjointed. Almann had stopped work on some new gadget and they'd eaten a hot meal for a change. The old man was more normal than usual, talking a lot and most of it sense.

The new power pile was working and Almann said craftily that now there was no chance that They would find him. Jason had never been sure who They were. Not the Stab, or at least not the part of the Stab he himself feared. Almann was quite different from the Pickers, like Arnie the tronman and himself. The old guy had been big up top, Versity, Jason was sure, but he thought something he knew was too much for the Marks, and he'd disappeared down here. First Jason had known of him was when he'd pounded open a meat can on an old rusted cut-off valve. The end had swung out of a battered tank sticking out of the wall and knocked him flat. Almann had dragged him in and threatened to kill him if he messed with the water supply again. The valve looked dead, rusted shut, but it had no guts and Almann drew gallons for his "work" which the boy had never fully understood. He had joined three old boiler shells, walled in and totally forgotten and rebuilt them into a first-class "lab", as he called it. It housed masses of stuff that the old man had swapped for special hand-made tools just for Pickers. Hadn't been so bad for Jason after that. He'd learned a lot when Almann was willing, some on his own when the old guy was lost in his work. He'd made it to where most tronlocks couldn't keep him from good pickings and he could even build some as good for pastime. What had they been doing, though? It blurred on him. and anyway enough time had gone by to let him take a look.

He barely cracked the door and listened. Nothing. A fraction more and he could see down the panel. Nothing! Yet apprehension was still with him. Whatever it was, it was somewhere out there waiting. He stepped out and moved to the metal door, palmed the lock with his "key", and slipped into the corridor. Something flickered at the right-angle half a block away and he was running again. This time he could hear footsteps behind him. He dodged through cross-passages and still it was there, a little closer. Down a ladder and across another corridor and he was almost home. He skidded to a halt alongside the unit and there was no panel. But this was his hole! He knew it! And there was no panel! The footsteps were louder again and panic took him. He ran blindly this time, but with the desperate cunning of the hunter hunted, in, out, up, down, doubling. Yet the pursuer drew closer and slowly, clearly, he began to hear the muted roar of the motorway. He turned parallel but found himself forced back. Nearer and inevitably nearer until, at last, before him was a small emergency exit off the motorway. Through it he could see the blurred stream of traffic, twelve lanes across, compelling, drawing, sucking him in. With his breath coming in huge, sobbing gasps, he forced himself to turn and look back, to face his nemesis. It was a huge figure, looming closer over him, but he couldn't seem to make out the features. In the naked fluoros an arm rose and from the clawed hand a belt swung, studded buckle flashing. Nick the Vert! Jason's heart pounded against his chest as the belt swung overhead.

He screamed endlessly, until his eyes suddenly snapped open and began to focus. The figure changed, grew smaller, and he realized it was Orest, holding him against the wall, yelling, "It's all right, Jason, it's all right." The room was bathed in light and he was standing pressed into a corner, feet braced into his mattress. Drawing a great, convulsive breath, he sagged down, out of Orest's grasp and shrank against his pillow, aware that it had been a nightmare, but shaking and drenched with sweat.

● ●

Morning brought Jason out of a still-troubled sleep, groggily trying to sift the shreds of frightening dreams from the reality of the past. Already the events of a mere yesterday seemed remote and fading. He made a strong effort to piece things together, slowly forming a more certain picture of the life he had known. People remained indistinct, but then, apart from Crazy Almann, he knew that he had dealt with them warily, briefly; intent on concealing his own hunting spots, patterns, hole, everything about himself, while he picked up information about techniques, Marks, the Stab, anything that was useful. Painfully, he reassembled the complex network of routes, layovers and hideaways that had been his territory in the sub-subjungle of Tor—Toronto. The name itself was an unimportant item. He forced himself to think back, trying to find some beginning, but events became hazy as he worked through a hodge-podge of similar days. Had he always known the hunt? Back before Almann it was even more indistinct, and he could feel a growing apprehension, sweat starting again as he probed. And there, finally, was one clear picture of a sobbing child, crouched at the end of a service conduit. Before that—something like a blank viewer screen. Shaken, he pushed the memory out of his mind, feeling all too vividly the utter loneliness of the child.

He was somewhat more alert now, though fatigue seemed to press him down. Through slitted eyes he noted that the shimmer of light still ran down the centre of the room, even with bright sunlight edging around his half of the curtained window. He returned to memory, testing for more recent events. Two days ago had been the same. He had bypassed two tronlocks and lifted a double handful of modules for Almann. The evening was clear too. The old man muttering to himself as he soldered with patient precision. Jason playing with the pirate micro-scanner, bored by the slowly passing lists of names under Econo-o-mics, Economics! He had turned instead to a sheaf of schematics. Yesterday was no different either, at least its beginning. He had dipped bread into a tin of strawberry—raspberry?—jam, planning a lift. Cable! He had been going to lift cable from—an open struction ramp over the motorway. And there, with a sharp sense of relief, he ran into the same blankness, shivering from unexplained dread.

There was a finality about those blanknesses which told him that it was useless to waste time and with the abruptness of those who move on the fringe of wipe-out, he turned to the present. Only what he needed today would be retrieved from the past and he faced his new situation with neither joy nor sorrow, only a deep-rooted will to live. He rolled stiffly off the bed and began to examine his room.

Suddenly, behind him the light wall was gone and he spun to face Orest, standing over his crumpled sleepsuit and scratching absently at his solid, hairy chest. Jason took in the heavy, smooth-muscled body, the athletic ease with which the young man moved and erased one possibility from the back of his mind. Orest draped a towel loosely about his hips and plucked a toilet kit from his cabinet, motioning Jason to do the same. "Guess we shouldn't push the schedule today," he said. "You'll want to flake early and catch up on your sleep. Good day for exams, though." He smiled reassuringly. "They go better when you're not too sharp. Keeps you from second-guessing, so your responses are true." He palmed open the door and threw back, "You want the best skill placement, so they'll be happy and you'll be happy

with your progress. Besides, skill credits are nice." He cut off abruptly
and Jason followed him down the corridor. Orest was surely saying
more than he should, had caught himself, but to the boy very little of
the whole made much sense.

It was a strange but exhilarating experience as he felt the coursing
water of a shower draw the stiffness from his body, and even more
enjoyable to use a cake of soap, working up a lather over his arms and
chest. He soon learned the use of a toothbrush (at least knew what a
comb was for) and watched as Orest shaved, leaving a faint blue behind in place of stubble. In the mirror Orest grinned. "You'll probably
not need one of these till you're shipped," he said. "Maybe not then.
I'm an old-fashioned safety razor man." He rinsed and opened the
instrument, showing Jason the parts and explaining the principle. The
boy twisted it shut, ran it over his cheek, found it hard to believe it
held a blade, until with widening eyes he looked at the welling cut on
his finger from grabbing the wrong end. He followed Orest back to
the room with blank face, sucking his finger, storing a useful bit of
information.

Jason welcomed the soft chime that announced breakfast. Together
they retraced the previous night's route, the boy filling in a near-
perfect visualization of this part of the complex, noting with an
uneasy feeling how few outer doors there were. He found himself
wondering what the sub-level layout was, where the hideouts would
be, but then, wryly, he set his mind firmly on breakfast and the
coming day.

The hall was full but strangely quiet. There was background music,
soft and full and peaceful. Any Musak Jason had caught from places
of concealment had kept the cruddy Marks scurrying. Here nobody
seemed rushed and yet they weren't wasting time. He and Orest
picked up trays and food, moved to the end of one long table, and
sat opposite another pair. Orest introduced himself and Jason to the
other young man who smiled and answered, "Ron and Mel." Then he
frowned slightly and said "Orest? Four years back? Ping-pong tourna-
ment." Orest thought briefly, then laughed. "Sure. You were in
Fraser Wing." Jason caught a minute impression of pain as Orest continued. "We must get together. Catch up." Then he turned the conversation, saying in a neutral voice, "We—Jason just came in last night."
He looked inquiringly at Mel, who stared back out of cold blue, bitter
eyes. Ron put a hand on the boy's shoulder and said with affection,
"This is an old-timer. Been here all of a month. Last trip to the dentist

this morning." Mel had gone rigid, fork in the air. Now he threw it down savagely and shoved his chair back. "I'm not finished yet," Ron spoke softly. The boy's face twisted with rage as he snarled, "To hell with you! To hell with this place, with everything!"

For a moment all conversation around them stopped, and Ron's voice came clearly but quietly over the muted music. "Sit down. Now." The boy's fists clenched and his throat worked as he threw a swift glance about him. For a brief span he stood taut and quivering, then slowly stepped back to the table and sat, tears of frustration spilling down his cheeks. He picked up his fork again, tines up and out. "Some day," he hissed without looking at Ron, "some day. I'll rip your guts out." Everything dropped back to normal so quickly around them that Jason had a fleeting notion that he must have dozed off and dreamed it. But Mel still sat, eating with vicious bites and though Ron was talking about something else there was a lurking, sad set to his mouth. Another item stored.

At booth 13 Orest explained the procedure. "The first part is written," he said, "and will show how well you can read. But put these phones on if the screen tells you. These buttons are for Yes and No, and these are numbered to four. Pick the answer that fits best. I'll be up front." Jason found the routine quite easy to adjust to, but very soon the words were becoming too difficult for him to mouth. After a particularly long wait, the screen said simply, "Put on your headphones." He did, and suddenly the pace of questioning accelerated, as a clear, smooth voice took over. He wanted to rest after the test on words, but there wasn't much time lapse before the screen lit up again and he was matching shapes, checking out the odd object in a group, setting up sequences. The screen went blank and he was answering a new kind of question. This is so, that is so, then is this so? The first few were childish, but then he caught himself being tricked. He picked up traps in the way things were worded, realized that his instinctive answer wasn't always right, in the pattern. He found himself disagreeing with first or second statements and he was relieved when the voice offered him a chance to reject any of them. It became an exciting challenge and when it ended he actually felt disappointed. Yet he was trembling with fatigue when Orest took the phones from his ears and kneaded the back of his neck. He blinked and made his eyes focus, then rolled drunkenly up the aisle after the young man, who had stopped again at the computer console. The machine extruded a long sheet of paper which Orest plucked out and studied. He had turned slightly away, but as Jason watched he could see the man's head slowly come up, until he was staring off into space. At last he turned back and said, rather carefully, "Well, Jason, you're no great shakes on reading. You'll pick that up soon enough, I imagine. Non-university personality set. Yet—160 IQ." He cleared his throat. "It's time for lunch now. We'll take a rest and go on this afternoon."

After eating with another pair much like Ron and Mel, they returned to their room, where Jason threw himself across his bed and dropped immediately into sleep. It seemed only minutes later that Orest was shaking him gently. He rolled irritably to the wall and dug his face into the pillow, muttering, "Lemme 'lone. Wanna sleep." But Orest became more insistent, finally seizing him under the armpits and sitting him firmly on the edge of the bed. "Come on," he said shortly. "Time to take the rest of your exams." Jason, temper flaring, snarled at him. "Tomorrow. I'll do 'em tomorrow. I'm too tired now." Orest stepped back and folded his arms across his chest. "You'll do them today! Or tonight! Or at three in the morning, if I say so!" he barked. "Now get on your feet." Jason's lip curled, but as he began to speak a vivid memory of Mel came into his mind. Surly, but obedient, he rose slowly and brushed long hair out of his face. "Straighten up your bunk, fast!" Orest prodded and once again defiance flared in the boy, and as he controlled it he felt it subside into smouldering resentment. He could easily come to hate this man, but it wouldn't be smart to let it show. Mulishly he spread out sheets and blanket, checking Orest's bed, but try as he might he couldn't make his as smooth and tight. Finally Orest showed him how, ending by dropping his scriber in the centre to see it bounce. "That's the way it will look every morning," he warned, "or you'll lose rec time remaking it. Now let's get moving."

And back they went to the exam room, where Jason spent the afternoon doing questions about heat, light, air, numbers and such, completely incomprehensible stuff about places and people he'd never known, and finally, schematics! As with the morning's exams, the last was fascinating and he wanted to go on even though the diagrams were becoming complex beyond anything he had worked with before. When it was over, he merely put his head down on the desk and searched for strength to move, while Orest went to the console and completed the evaluations. He couldn't protest when he was physically lifted from his chair and led to the dining hall.

Through bloodshot eyes he acknowledged the presence of yet

another pair, while he mechanically stuffed food into his mouth. He barely noticed the people scattered through the lounge, relaxing with various pastimes, on his way to their room. Bed was a pit of welcome oblivion and he was asleep before he could give a thought to the day past.

Sometime during the night Jason could recall having half-wakened, driven upward towards consciousness by nightmare, but it seemed not to have lasted as long and he had sunk back into sleep after a few fitful starts. This time he had a vague recollection of hanging outward over a wall, caught by the backs of his knees, while a large, blurred figure threatened and the motorway thundered far below. Then he was falling slowly downward, towards the rushing traffic, until he woke. Despite the one interruption he must have slept well, for he felt alert and rested, ready for whatever Orest might inflict upon him.

That stalwart was once again up and stretching, stifling an enormous yawn as he stripped the bedclothes from his bunk and motioned Jason to do the same. The boy got the job of taking clothes and linen to the launderit and after eating they picked up the clean laundry. He did a passable job of making his bed, somehow anxious to match Orest, then they were off to tour the school complex, marvellous in its scope and compactness. Labs and shops of every description were arranged in the central area near the dining hall. Sleeping wings radiated from this hub, and between them were open areas and a "gym", where it seemed one could play at all those things the Marks loved watching on vidscreens. There was even a building with hockey rink and curling sheets—which had been too far beyond his daily fight to survive to capture his interest. He was dazed by the immense gulf between his past life and what lay before him, frightened by the sudden realization that he would be expected to take part, that most of the people here must use all these. For the first time, he began to wonder what the others had done to be trapped here, what he had done. Nevertheless, a wary corner of his mind noted that the shape of all Orest had shown him was a semi-circle: the layout was clear, every room and corridor from his wing—Lacombe?—to the farthest, MacKenzie Wing, which was on a straight line right through the central complex. And what did that mean? There were no discernible exits to the other half of the circle. Store it!

When they returned, shortly before lunch, Orest showed him how to fold back the top of his desk and pull out a scanner. He went over the instruction manual carefully, dialling microfilm and tapes from the library, showing Jason the reading aid attachment. "I'll have a programme for you tomorrow morning," Orest smiled. "According to how fast you go, there'll be adjustments made. For now," he added, "you'll do what I think you need. I don't think you'll have to read all morning, somehow. Once you get that skill out of the way you'll spend time in the labs. And there's PhysEd too—got to put meat on them bones." He laughed at that and as the chime sounded they went to lunch.

Jason had found himself wondering about this whole setup. The Stab had said he was guilty of some big trip, but so far he couldn't see where the hook was. Bread, a sweet hole, a chance maybe to dig 'tronics; it sure wasn't the wipeout he'd expected from listening to the other Pickers. But back in the room he got his first taste of the hook. As soon as they'd closed the door a panel above it slid back and a long buzz drilled his ears. Behind the panel was a scanner which showed simply—Lenchuk Berkley: KP area 2: 6/24—7/10. Orest sighed and pressed a button in the top of the door frame. "Well," he murmured, "they still get you moving right off. We've got sixteen days of KP, starting now."

It was hot, despite the climatrol, and Jason had never worked so hard in his life. Pile after pile of dirty cups, plates and cutlery was racked and sent through the washers. His utility suit clung to him and he took small comfort from the fact that two other boys, faces drawn and sweat-beaded, worked alongside him. Behind them, Orest and two other men were checking out belts and loaders and through one of the belt accesses Jason caught a glimpse of two others working in the more familiar area behind the serving doors. He had raided that section in more than one autoteria and he wondered now if there had been anyone in the next room, doing what he now slaved at. No: there would have been more noise. Must have been robos.

With a groan of relief he helped to send the last rack into the washer and squatted down to rest. "All right!" Orest called out, "stack 'em!" With incredulous anger, he turned to see Orest pointing to the empty loaders. The other boys had already begun to clear the hot racks and Jason followed, inwardly seething. One more point against the big crud, he thought, letting anger sweep through his body to give him strength. It had not left him when he loaded the last pod of knives and they methodically mopped the floor right to the entry, so he called up images of himself standing over a sweating Orest, mopping with a toothbrush. It nearly made him smile. His back ached and his fingers were puffy, his face felt oily and his hair was stiff, but when they had showered and had supper he was still alive enough to go into the lounge with Orest and watch for a while. Most games didn't interest him much. He might learn to play some day, just to see if he could beat these Marks. The one with the funny pieces though, that looked promising. He could see an infinity of corridors on the chessboard, could see that some of the pieces, just like the Marks, had to stick to certain patterns. Only one big piece could go anywhere it pleased. He found himself remembering the levels of the city he had known. Yes, this was a game for him. When Orest, answering, said he played, Jason noted a slight caution, a veiling of the eyes, and after that he knew the man was watching, thinking.

As he bedded down for the night, the boy mulled over everything he had learned in the past two days. Life here had its bad qualities, like Orest, who was still up and prowling the other side of the light wall. That kitchen work too, and probably crud like it—they might have a number of unpleasant surprises for him. Well, he had some surprises for them too. If they thought they were going to break him, Orest included, they were dead wrong. He could take that slop every afternoon and morning too, for that matter. There'd come a time, meanwhile, when he would find the way out. And if he got into the labs, he'd leave a little present for the big crud too, when he busted. It was a pleasant way to drift into sleep and his night was completely untroubled at last.

It was fantastic how time seemed to fly after that. Jason moved from one thing to the next so quickly that he had little time, except in the private moments before sleep, to puzzle over what was happening to him. He had picked up his reading with very little trouble and even Orest was impressed, which gave the boy a bitter kind of satisfaction. But the young man gave him little praise and a hell of a lot more work for his reward. He had taken quite naturally to the sciences, and would have spent all of his time at the scanner on that part of his programme, but the ever-present Orest would look up from his own work, check the time and pry him loose sometimes almost physically, to make him work on history, geography, sociology and a batch of garbage. He hated languages and won only the small concession from his tormentor that he could use phones and take a dose late in the evenings, so long as he could pass the weekly quizzes.

It was the same with other activities too. He actually liked gymnastics and he knew that someday he would pass Orest, in fact leave him far behind. Even now, on the bars and rings, he was performing better than boys years older. But team sports he couldn't stand. There was a barrier between him and the other boys which he himself created, he knew, since most of them got on with one another, but he couldn't bring himself to do anything about it and they didn't make much of an effort either. In the lounge he played only games against a single opponent, with a fierce concentration and graceless exultation over winning that soon left him few takers. Orest had remarked on it when they sat playing chess one evening, while most of the others were at a baseball game in the late summer sunshine. "You know," he had mused, "there's a lot more to life than being top man in games." Jason had snorted derisively at him. "What more is there in this cage?" he retorted. Orest had sat back and looked at him sadly, obviously seeking words. In the end he had merely said cryptically, "Until you get *that* monkey off your back, there isn't anything more."

But with summer gone, and the dusk settling at 20:00, and then 19:00, he got his chance at the labs and he couldn't have cared less about his social life. Orest had to tear him away and finally requested that they be assigned to evening labour, in order to give him more time in the day. It was then, too, that Jason had his first real look at the world outside the school, although he was still inside a fence. They went to harvest, working among the combines and trucks and he was overwhelmed by the vast, sweeping fields of grain, stretching out towards the dusty foothills, framed by the purple haze of mountains. The sheer space was unbelievable. A strange emotion woke in him, one which he couldn't define, but which brought tears to his eyes when he stopped to rest and look. They worked on into the darkness each night, the combines lumbering glaring-eyed across the sections of school land. Then one night it was over. The combines lurched out a great gate, were taken by strange drivers and moved on, leaving the inmates to clear off, fill the last granaries and go back to school. It was the pigbarns and dairy next for Jason and Orest, where automation or not the work was still hard for the boy, and Orest, ever-watchful, made checks and repairs.

Perhaps it was winter, perhaps his imagination, but as time wore on it seemed to Jason that Orest was becoming more and more oppressive. Just when he was settling into a routine that suited him perfectly, Orest had switched it around. He had wanted to stick with the tron-lab, fascinated by the possibilities it presented, when Orest announced that he must move to physics. He had bitten back angry words and set about mastering his lessons with vicious drive. Then Orest had told him he was going to study literature in the mornings and when he furtively dialled a film on trontraffic, the cruddy bum had wired a limiter to his selector. The last straw came when he put the gym off limits.

It wasn't much of a fight, really. Orest stood impassively in the centre of the room and repeated carefully, "The gym is out of bounds. You're going to the hockey rink." Jason was incredulous. "Ah, come off it, Orest. I can't even skate, for crissakes," he pleaded. But his custodian simply folded his arms, mouth in a thin, straight line. "What are ya tryin' to do to me?" Jason's voice rose. "You're takin' away everything I like, everything I want." Even more shrilly, he shouted, "You're jealous, damn you. You know I'm good, better than you are—better than you'll ever be, you lousy crud." On the last his voice broke and it came out in a wailing falsetto that shattered his remaining control. In a blind fury he rolled off the bed, fists flailing, only to find himself pushed back hard enough to bounce off the mattress, against the wall and down on to the bed again. Shaking his head, he launched himself at Orest, who grabbed him in mid-air, swung him around and bounced him even harder off the wall. With animal rage, Jason drove for the other's legs, found empty air, and slid head first into the cabinets under Orest's bunk. Nearly unconscious, he managed to sit up, blood streaming down both sides of his nose from a cut on his forehead. He tried to get his feet under him, sat down heavily again and shook uncontrollably. He watched helplessly as Orest took a facecloth and left, returning to wipe his face and utility suit and hold the cloth to his head. He was carried to his own bunk and dropped, and as he lay face down, shaking from the emotional storm, he listened to his custodian.

"It took a long time, Jase, longer than most, but it came." Orest paused, hoping the boy would understand. "It always does, they say. Even with a genius." He sighed heavily. "I don't think you need the medic. And you're going to learn to skate. You'll play hockey if it kills both of us." He rose and stripped off Jason's suit, not roughly, pulled the sheet and blanket from under the boy and covered him. Jason, crushed and humiliated, retreated somewhere deep within himself to nurse a cold, steely hate. He lay awake for a long time that night, thinking, planning, and finally slept.

● ● ●

He did learn to skate. His fine balance and sinewy leanness made it surprisingly easy and good skating enabled him to play passable hockey with the others, most of whom had had a stick and puck before they could walk. Nevertheless, he played with a singleness of purpose which kept it from being sport with him. His lightness made him vulnerable too, and no matter what team he played with, his opponents seemed to relish catching him with a bruising check or a shoulder along the boards. Still, he didn't retaliate. You don't score in the penalty box. And at least Orest and the other men were scrupulously fair about refereeing the games.

He was careful to do everything he was told, now, and seemed completely indifferent to changes in his programme. Orest had an uncanny ability to spot his growing enthusiasm for a subject and several times thwarted him again, but he was determined not to let his frustrations show. Common sense had told him that sooner or later he must return to some things, that very few subjects had been more than opened up for him. Just after Christmas, a meaningless respite, he got his chance to return to the tronlab. It was the one thing he had been waiting for, not merely because he had an all-consuming interest in it, but because he had a long-considered plan in mind.

To even a sharp-eyed observer it would have appeared that Jason was following out reasonably circumscribed projects: constructing model trontraffic controls, authorized computer circuits, standard test equipment, at times playing with his own refinements and demonstrating them to Orest, who clearly had other specializations. That in itself gave him a sadistic satisfaction, having a labtech praise his work while Orest looked on, not quite following. But in the brief time he allowed himself after completing a project, before checking out, he stole a moment for the all-important thing. First it was a casual touch of screwdriver to the face of that detestable plate in his arm, with its shimmering *Dependence.* He'd never seen Orest's clearly, but it surely didn't say that! On the first try he got only a tingle. Next day, with a "slip", he numbed his whole arm. What was the difference? Touching the centre gave the least effect, but closer to the edges he could nearly put himself out. Adding it up, he recognized a peripheral force field. The cruddy Stab probably had it rigged to destruct if anyone tried to remove it for you.

The plate itself, he had long since deduced, was a combination sensor and transceiver. Just from the advanced equipment he was using here, he knew they could monitor and control as many circuits as they wanted in a unit that size. He'd seen a beauty almost as small in a tape on the Mars landing team, grafted between the shoulder-blades. And what did it amount to, after all, but a sophisticated version of something he had worked over often enough. He could visualize the circuitry closely enough for his purpose. His concern was not with the device itself, but with a counter-device. And here he had experience to draw on. It had been a long time since he first sat in a corner at Almann's, cannibalizing an old, useless "key". Painfully drawing out the schematic, he had rebuilt it, with a minor modification of his own that Almann had absent-mindedly OK'd. He'd built more than one since then, each one better than the last, until he was able to open most regular tronlocks he'd run up against. A key was, essentially, a jammer, and that was what he wanted now—a jammer to cut him off completely from the Stab when the time finally came. Yet this one had to invert rather than broadcast, or they could spot him just as easily. It was a problem that occupied every free moment until he achieved a breakthrough, for it had to be right the first time.

So the months passed into March, while he carefully slipped in the occasional experiment with micro-circuitry. He secured and reused a small oval watchcase, left it lying in the drawer of his bench, and each time carried a tiny submodule back to his room in the toe of his utility suit. Piece by piece, crafted with jeweller's perfection, the unit was designed and constructed, until nothing but the power seed was missing from the pile just inside the bottom of Jason's scanner frame. Finally he got that too, when he turned in a "defective" and retrieved it with a wet fingertip as he held the new one up to the light to hold the stockman's eye. Orest had been right behind him, and it filled Jason with unholy glee as the two men searched for the missing seed. They'd find it all right, on the floor in front of the counter, but it was a useless grain of graphite strung on a hairwire, identical in appearance to the real thing.

Three days later he assembled the jammer, every part fitting perfectly into the case, and wired the stem to the seed. On the bench was a minituway receiver showing a steady output. Three types of sensitive detector were on in the bank of test equipment, covering the whole communication spectrum. He took a deep breath and pulled out the stem. Not a needle trembled. Casually he cupped the case under his palm and placed it over the tuway. The output meter dropped to zero. With his free hand he switched to transmit, flipped the dial of the meter and watched. Still nothing. He depressed the watchstem. The meter jumped to full output. Shakily, Jason put both fists to the neck of his suit and pushed his elbows back, stretching. The case slipped down his chest, across his twitching stomach muscles, down his leg and against the arch of his foot. An hour later he turned in his project and sauntered back to his room with Orest, innocently chewing at a scrap length of plastic.

It should have made up for the growing friction between himself and the other boys, the gnawing rebelliousness over Orest's constant meddling with his programme, his demands for absolute obedience. He had held all his frustrations at arm's length, curiously like a disinterested spectator. But in the early morning, wide awake, he tossed in his bunk as the full measure of his grievances closed in. Instead of peace, in the certain knowledge that he now possessed the means of escape, resentment and half-thoughts of vengeance raised in him the torments of the persecuted. The next morning he refused to study the material set out for him. Orest, patience long exhausted, snapped out, "No study, no food! Bread and milk until you smarten up!" Jason all but radiated white heat as he turned to the scanner and balefully stared at the unrolling pages of gibberish.

Orest watched in grim silence, slammed his scriber across the desk and stalked out to the bathroom. Jason waited, stiff-backed, counting seconds. At fifteen he rose quietly, slipped across and opened Orest's cabinet. Quickly he reached in and unzipped the toilet kit, thumbed a razor blade out of the dispenser, replaced everything as before and sat down in front of his scanner again. The blade went with the plastic and watchcase, inside the scanner frame. For the rest of the day he was docile, to the point where Orest seemed to be suspicious, so he made a point of arguing with the other over chess in the lounge that evening. It nearly backfired, as the boiling emotions he had submerged for so long threatened to erupt, but he managed to hold on to himself. He made a familiar enough picture, standing white-faced and hollow-eyed over the scattered pieces, slowly buckling to submission under the authority of his custodian. Others shrugged off the common occurrence and Orest seemed to accept it as a return to the hateful norm. Later, behind the light wall, Jason sat at his desk again, scanner humming at normal speed and cut a strap for his watchcase from the length of plastic. Then, with deft care, he sliced through half the thickness of the remaining plastic at one end, almost to the width of the blade. There he left it embedded. He slipped the short piece of plastic between third and fourth fingers and clenched his fist, noting with grim satisfaction the edge of the blade ran the length of fingers from knuckle to first joint. It was a nasty weapon, deadly if used precisely. Watching and listening to the other Pickers had taught him many things.

He was ready. And small comfort it seemed to bring. In the morning, with quiet confidence, he had taped a "blister" on his heel and furtively slipped his small weapon into the foot of his suit. The feeling of smug pleasure had lasted through study session and lab, but somehow he felt all the more vulnerable in the late afternoon, when he stripped and put on his hockey equipment. Skating by himself at one end of the rink, while the others went through stupid drills and skull sessions with the men, he whipped the puck at the boards, but could not capture his usual savage pride at the pin-point accuracy. He found himself wondering why he was always with the older, heavier boys when there were others his own age. He seemed to take more and more physical punishment lately: everyone seemed to enjoy racking him up. Well, he could take it and sometimes made them look like stupid Marks when he got away for a clean shot on goal.

But today it seemed harder than ever and it began to get to him. To make matters worse, twice he took what should have been obvious fouls and no one called them. During a shift when his line was on the bench, he suddenly realized that it had been Mel, dumb Mel, who had got him both times. Back on the ice again he concentrated on getting the puck and when at last it came sliding out of a mixup near his own goal, he hooked it under his blade and picked up speed. Flashing down the right wing he finessed the defenceman and closed on the goalie. From the corner of his eye he caught movement, but the shot was there to be made. Wrists cocked, he feinted towards the lower stickside, saw the goalie commit himself, had the whole upper glove side of the net to aim at. And incredibly, a knee came up into his groin, a heavy body smashed into his left side, and he was spinning through the air. He lay at a grotesque angle, watched as there was a minute pause among his teammates and gaped as play went on. A grinning, taunting Mel arced by him and moved out, as his forwards carried a three-man break to the far end. Jason somehow made it to the bench, tears stinging in the cold at the injustice of it. Grossly unfair! That he had never held the concept before meant nothing. He was washed by a mind-sapping wave of rage.

The game was over before he could get back on the ice again, but this time he could not set it to one side. In the dressing room he stopped before his locker and waited for Mel to come by. Around him, the happy buzz of after-game razzing began, while he dropped stick and gloves, drew off his shirt and unlaced hip-pads. Mel came alone, between the benches, a superior sneer aimed just for Jason and the boy stuck a hand out at his chest. "You fouled me," he hissed. "Three times!" The other stopped, sturdy on his skates, and smiled innocently at the rest. "Me?" he asked. "I didn't hear any whistles. Did you guys?" There were mutters, some agreeing and a few non-committal. Reassured, Mel grinned again. "Besides," he snickered, "what could you do about it, star?" Without thinking, without warning, Jason caught Mel flush on the nose, staggering him for a second. The youngster's eyes widened as he grabbed his nose and found blood on his hands, and with a strangled bellow he charged forward, skates thumping. By sheer weight he knocked Jason back into the open locker and all reason fled. Groping under him, the boy reached into the foot of his suit and clutched his plastic strap. He came up swinging as the group of players fell back. Once, twice, the wicked blade sliced, opening up Mel's shirt, baring the stuffing in his shoulder-pad, and as numbness struck, turning his bones to jelly, Jason found himself lifted off the floor in a crushing embrace. A babble of excited voices rose round him as Orest, holding him with one arm, plucked the blade out of his loose fingers and then flung him down on the bench. Everything came back into focus with chilling clarity, as one thought pounded through Jason's brain. Blown! He had blown it!

What he had expected, Jason couldn't say, but in retrospect it looked not too bad. He and Orest had sat for hours in the great hall, waiting silently until they were summoned to the indoctrination chamber. There the same three men had appeared, looking and sounding more severe than before. "Jason Berkley," the first said harshly, "consider the seriousness of these charges. Carrying a concealed weapon. Armed assault. Deadly intent. Do you deny any of these?" Jason was bursting with the urge to shout out the injustice of it, to tell how he had been provoked. But he knew that appearances were against him and he remained silent, looking downward. "You are at present not under civil jurisdiction," the voice continued, "or major punishment would be exacted. Instead, you are barred from the environs, rights and privileges of this school until such time as you are found fit to return." The second man addressed Jason. "In the eight months that you have enjoyed the unique opportunities afforded by this institution," he said in an even more grave tone, "you have made astonishing progress in your programme. We have twice revised your productivity potential upward. Your usefulness to society is unquestionable. However, you have shown no progress in social adaptability. If this does not improve radically, since you have nearly exhausted the tolerance factor, it will be economically unfeasible to allow you more resources."

Mumbo-jumbo, Jason thought, but he could grasp the threat. It meant that they would erase him; give him a wipe-out. Then the last spoke. "As with all human relations," he said sadly, "there is much under the surface to explain your actions. We are aware of circumstances beyond your violence. Nevertheless, you cannot remain as a disturbing influence. You will be sent to seclusion, to pursue a more rigorous programme under absolute supervision. Stand back!" Jason shuffled towards the door as Orest stepped forward. "Orest Lenchuk! You are not a skilled psychologist, yet sections of your bibliography should have been attended with care. Note those on sibling association and particularly the complications of rising Oedipus manifestation. I need not stress the consequences of failure." He closed a small scanner and snapped out the cassette, as the TriVid cubicle went dead.

April first! "You're sixteen today," Orest had commented bitterly as they slung their meagre possessions into the roboflit. "Sixteen, and you're a disaster looking for a place to happen." They had settled into silence, bundled in parkas against the sharp cold. From his side, Jason watched the country change beneath them as they raced westward, parallelling a barely discernible roadbed to the north. They had left even the vast ranchlands behind and were moving bumpily across unbroken forest, through air currents roughed by the foothills ranging north and south. In the distance the mountains grew taller until it seemed that they should reach them any moment. Finally they towered over the craft in awesome, naked splendour, threatening to spill down the masses of snow from their upper reaches. Yet for all their intimidation Jason ignored them and as they descended towards a narrow, flat strip in a shallow valley he tasted a fraction of triumph. In his toilet kit, at the bottom of the duffel bag they shared, was the watchcase that Orest had missed when he searched Jason's side of the room back at school.

They dumped the bag into waist-deep snow and stood gasping in biting wind until the roboflit took off. Then, with Orest breaking a path, they made their way to a crude, solid cabin. If Jason had begun to see his early life in Toronto as bare survival, this was calculated to make it seem like luxury. There was a startling contrast between the two small, remote scanners and the split-pole desks they sat on, between the vidscreen in the wall and the huge woodstove next to it, between the shelves of compact foodpacks and the metal bucket and pan beneath them. Leaving the bag on the floor, Orest took a ring of flat metal keys and fitted one into a door. It opened into a small room containing hand tools, shovels, a locked rack of guns and a sealed power unit. Hefting a broad axe, Orest locked the door and headed outside, calling curtly to Jason to follow. If they were ever to warm up they must cut wood for the stove. It was a gentle introduction to New Eden.

· Actually, the basic chores proved almost a joy to Jason, no matter how they taxed his strength and endurance. Anything was better than the battle that evolved inside. Day after day, Jason was subjected to a constant stream of commands, corrections, abuse. Nothing he did pleased Orest and he found himself repeating simple exercises, rereading endless amounts of social history, ferreting out the smallest details of literature until, sometime in the early morning hours, the relentless figure would point and he would drag himself to his bunk. The only consolation was that if it was tearing him to pieces it was nearly as hard on Orest, who was looking gaunt and hollow-cheeked. Jason knew that he was doing his own studying too, had even wakened briefly to hear him talking indistinctly at the vidscreen and wondered if he might yet win, if Orest were slowly losing his grip. He had to win! If he lost, a soul-destroying chasm yawned at his feet.

As the first days of May came and went, he was running on some unfathomed reserve deep in his being and it was almost gone. In one morning's sunlight he took a huge breath of chilly air and found that he could not, would not return to the cabin. They were out to cut wood again for the great rusty monster that swallowed cords at a time. Or at least Orest did the cutting while Jason carried and stacked. They both knew too well what Jason would use the axe for, and with stunning simplicity, a quirk of fate, Jason's burden was lifted. One moment he stood captive and the next Orest was flat on his back, felled by a bullet-like chip that blurred off the biting axe blade from the deep vee of the log.

Not quite that simple, for Orest never completely lost his hold on the axe. But he weaved and swayed as he groped for a tree trunk, his lids kept closing over blank eyes and his speech was thick as he waved a heavy arm, beckoning Jason to help. Cunning stirred in the boy as he moved slowly to assist, putting his shoulder under the other's arm and guiding him. He might grab the axe and get Orest in one sweeping chop, but it was risky. Attack might rouse him enough to fend it off. Better to wait. At the cabin, Orest steered them doggedly to the store-room, fishing with clawed fingers for his key ring. Dropping the axe inside, he locked the door and stumbled to his bunk. Jason dipped a cloth into water and placed it on the side of his companion's head, where a swelling, ugly bruise showed through matted, bloody hair. He calculated the risk as he held the cloth in place and Orest hovered on the edge of passing out. He could do it now, in one of several ways. But to his disgust some vaguely similar incident from the past woke in memory and he found himself discarding the idea, rationalizing it away. After all, if he shouldn't make it, killing Orest was a sure ticket to a wipe-out.

Reluctantly he straightened Orest's legs and left him lying on his side, cloth beneath his head. He was breathing heavily, but it looked as if he'd sleep it off. Jason stripped the blankets from his bed and rolled them, crammed as many foodpacks into the duffel bag as it would hold and strapped the mass into a bundle, leaving loops to slip over shoulders. Quickly he filled a water container, tied it and a pot to the bundle and stuffed a box of matches into an inner pocket. Last he took the watchcase from his kit and strapped it on over the plate in his arm, reading that damned *Dependence* with humourless irony. The tingling hit an intensity just short of numbing his whole right side, but his heart thudded triumphantly when he pulled the stem and instantly the tingling stopped. Massaging his arm, he stepped through the door and was gone.

The roadbed had run to the north of them, at the end of a series of small connecting valleys. Where there was a roadbed there were robo-freights and someplace was a layover. There was probably a motorway too, he thought, with that faint queasiness that the image always brought, but not this side of the roadbed. Two or three days should get him there and the weather was good. Brilliant sunshine threw a dazzling reflection off the patches of melting snow as he made his way through light cover along a creek bank. He made good time even when he was forced to climb, breaking through heavier timber at the end of the valley. The sun moved across his left shoulder and plunged behind a rocky summit, leaving Jason in that sudden, thickening twilight which he had barely noticed before. With a light breeze in his face, he pushed forward until he could hardly see, finally fetching up in a tiny clearing under an overhanging face of granite. There he built a fire, ate a foodpack and drank. For a complete novice he managed surprisingly well, even arranging his fire so that it burned slowly and evenly until near morning. Yet when he wakened he found his feet and hands were lightly frost-bitten. The temperature had dropped well below freezing, close to −20C, and until he rebuilt his fire it was painful to move.

He ate sparingly and moved off at a fast pace, the wind more brisk now and the sky overcast. The going was rough too, and he wound up boxed at the end of a canyon near noon. He had only made it across a ridge and down into the next valley when night fell again, accompanied by a sifting of dry, loose snow. It was brutally cold now and he huddled for hours, dozing fitfully, until he finally fell into a troubled sleep sitting up. A piercing scream brought him awake, trembling with cold and fright, almost too stiff to move as he stared into the darkness beyond the embers. Off to the right there was a coughing sound and he knew some predator was stalking. It was sheer agony to stir, but he shoved twigs and then some small branches into the coals and slowly brought back a flickering ring of light around him. Then in the stillness came another disturbing sound. High above him the wind was moaning through the trees and all about him was the hiss of falling snow.

By morning the wind was howling, driving solid sheets of snow into his eyes. The footing was treacherous in the undergrowth that whipped across his face and tore at his pack, for the little gulleys were filling in, inviting the step that would plunge him hip-deep. Wet, clinging snow soaked through his leggings, his parka, until it seemed to lie against his flesh and freeze it to the bone. The wind had changed. He came on tracks, spun about, and realized that they were his own. And the temperature was plunging below zero. He fell once, got up and pushed on, fell again, got up again, knew that his fingers in the mitts were sticks of ice. Many falls later he couldn't get back up and it was easier, much easier to lie there drowsing, slipping off into . . . He brought his head up by a tremendous effort, opened his eyes caked shut by snow and crawled. Around the next trunk and into the next hollow. Pulling himself along a little slope he rolled over on his back, arms and legs splayed without control, looking upward at the unfocussed face far above him. Faintly he mouthed the words that should have come long ago: "Help me, Orest, help me."

Another April first. Eighteenth birthday. He had been right, back there in the bush cabin, for it *had* meant the end of the old Jason Berkley. The new Jason, however, had found freedom in submission, a marvellous world which held more than he could ever embrace in his great hunger for life, for experience. After Orest had hauled him back an excruciating ten miles to complete the great circle he'd run, he'd come to know true dependence. For weeks he had lain motionless, fever coursing through him, dependent upon Orest for life itself. And later, he had found himself unable to do the slightest task, make the smallest decision, without Orest's guidance. The most brilliant accomplishment was without meaning or pleasure unless Orest approved.

Of course it couldn't go on that way. But Orest had given him what he needed unstintingly, given so much of himself that they were closer than father and son, or brothers. And the immense rewards had grown day by day to fill him with never-ceasing wonder. The studies which he had undertaken at the start were the merest fundamentals. With Orest to explain, suggest, he had mastered and enjoyed the full range of his programme. More important, he could count as friends all the boys in his wing and a host of others. He and Orest had moved to paired sports, mixed groups, and he could talk respectfully to the other men, receiving warm courtesy in return.

His seventeenth birthday had been a step forward too, for he had found out what made up the other half of the circle—the mirror half of his, save that it housed girls. Frightening at first, they were, until he saw that some of them were just as apprehensive as he was. He still hadn't been comfortable, but as Orest pointed out they made up half the world. Eventually Orest had given him a choice: take them or leave them. But he knew Orest was pleased when he doubled with him on weekend evenings. When sex education had been added to his programme it had become acutely embarrassing, seeing these creatures with double vision, so-to-speak, as biological organisms and as feeling, thinking human beings. It had finally penetrated that he was really being prepared for the outside world. The idea was shocking, but he now wondered at how naive he could be, when all the clues had been there from the start.

The outside world indeed. This morning he and Orest had been summoned to the great hall again. They had stood in front of the door to the indoctrination chamber and Jason noticed that he was taller than Orest, though still lighter. Shoulder to shoulder they had faced the TriVid cube, charged with excitement. The ceremony was over so quickly that Jason felt a bit cheated. The same three men had appeared, greyer, or was it his imagination?

"Jason Berkley," announced the first, "you have completed Phase One and, coincidentally, achieved majority. By so much, the law is satisfied." Immediately the second said, "You will now be given the productivity which will eventually repay society's investment. You will be sent to the metropolis of Edmonton, where you have been assigned a job as electonics design engineer. This is a high-skill position, with accompanying high-credit deposits. After deductions against repayment of debt, you will have sufficient to rate a stretched ELS, and one has been rented for you." The third man had leaned forward and said with a minute hint of warmth, "Such an Efficiency Living Space denotes status in the world you are entering. Do not be misled. This is still a learning situation and the ledger is far from balanced." He paused and watched the puzzled Jason. "You are free, for the time being, to make your own way. Peace and unity be within you. Please wait outside." Orest stepped forward as Jason left.

Now it was afternoon and he was looking forward with mixed feelings to his future. "Sorry to keep you waiting," Orest called as he entered the hall. He was carrying a case identical to that at Jason's feet, and a package under his arm. Smiling broadly, he handed the package to the tall young man, who unwrapped it with happy wonder. "I notice a little fuzz, Jase," Orest chuckled, "and it might not go down well with the women." It was a razor like Orest's and Jason's throat clogged as memories, good and bad, swept through his mind. The older man turned him towards the door as he slipped an AP Card into his hand. The heavy doors slid silently back, to some unseen bidding, and they stepped together into spring sunlight. As Orest entered a robocar he waved and offered a last word of advice. "Roll your sleeve up, Jase, and take a look. Work hard and know yourself best of all. See you." With that he was gone, and Jason gazed at the metal plate in his tingling arm. Beneath its surface shimmered— *Independence.*

● ● ● ●

Edmonton should have seemed relatively small and uncomplicated, with a mere million inhabitants, yet Jason found his apprehensions had been at least partly justified. He had come in by monorail from Red Deer, near the school, and the trip had been pleasant until the last few minutes, when he'd watched the gap narrow between himself and the motorway stretching back to Calgary. The hairs had risen on the backs of his arms and neck, under his new swagger suit, as he watched northbound traffic beneath, moving nearly as fast as their own 200 kph. Even moving along the pedexpress to Leacock Manor, his new home, he felt vaguely uncomfortable, as if after all this time he should still be somewhere prowling the sub-levels. The lobby of the Manor was no help either. He'd been escorted to the office by a supercilious and disapproving manager, obviously put out at having to come and open to his ring.

Safe in his own ELS, he had looked about at the decor, in the same garish taste as that of the lobby and decided that no amount of fatalism could make him accept it. Changes would be made when he could afford them. Meanwhile, he needed time to familiarize himself with the most basic routines. Orest had prepared him and yet he fumbled and hesitated over many little things. Using his AP Card, he dialled a menu, lingered over it, and chose his meal. He went to bed with a late newsfax and read every line—especially the ads.

Morning brought him early to the gates of Western Safety Electronics, Ltd., where the roboguard checked him through Security and took him to the office of J. T. Monihan, design manager. Jason's AP Card went into a slot by his desk scanner and a cassette into the other side. Without comment Monihan read carefully and completely till, with a grunt, he tossed Jason's AP Card back. Startled, Jason dropped it into an ashtray, where a cigar curled fragrant smoke upward. He jerked the card out, flushing, while the grey-haired, steely-eyed Monihan reached forward and retrieved his stogey. "Damn things are indestructible," he said in a deceptively mild voice. "Don't suppose they told you that at Diamond Willow." Jason reddened again, but the stocky, middle-aged man waved a casual hand. "Seen 'em all," he said. "The EVR boys who haven't left their own homes since they started courses. Videotape for brains. The red-hot grad-schoolers, gonna turn our organization upside down. And one or two like you . . . or at least from your school." He looked sharply at Jason. "Says here you're cleared to level three security. Pretty far for wet ears. Says, too, that you're really high-skill." He paused, waiting for a reaction, and continued when he got none. "Well, doesn't matter here anyway. Got great new designs to show me? Keep 'em. Everyone starts on the line. Know the plant, follow the system from start to finish and maybe someday you'll get your scriber back."

He obviously expected a comeback and seemed almost disappointed when Jason merely nodded. "All right, then," he said as he butted his cigar. "I'll give you the grand tour." He moved with exceptional grace for one his shape and size. Jason stayed one step behind until Monihan turned and took his arm. "Come on," he growled, "you're not with the ancient Royal Family." They strode along in silence until they reached the entrance to a huge room where rows of figures sat hunched over long benches. Down the centre of the first few, conveyor belts moved silently and in the background was a pleasant sound not quite like music. They stopped at the end of the first row and Monihan stabbed a stubby finger forward. "Assembly line," he said quietly. "Bread and butter." He picked up a partly-finished piece. "Standard citizen's electronic lock. Frequency keyed. Made by the million and jimmied by the thousand." They moved on. "Luxury lock," he intoned. "Voice pattern keyed. Takes a multi-frequency scrambler to jimmy. Also takes multi-credits to purchase." Jason had known only one Picker with the know-how and equipment to get past one of those.

Now they were at the end of a bench with no belt. Monihan reached past a woman intent on her work and picked up an oblong case, about one inch by a half, wafer thin. "You're a micro-circuitry specialist. Attaché case lock. Thumbprint keyed." He gestured towards a glassed room where a roboguard prowled restlessly. "Personal fitting." There were similar items at the next benches, some clearly for vanity rather than security. A key in a diamond neckcloth pin, a lock in a hot water button, for a safe beneath the basin. "Some characters have more credits than brains, even today," the manager quipped sarcastically.

"We also do priority AP Card locks," he continued. "Only two other firms have that clearance from the Continental Computer people. And you've heard of our ultra-special lock, for the Americanadian Government. The one-of-a-kind with three keys, in Washington, Ottawa and Hemisphere Defence?" Jason hadn't. Monihan swung around and looked down the room. "You've seen all you're cleared for," he finished. "This afternoon you start on the first belt and you do every operation in this room to my satisfaction before you set foot in my design section. It can take three months or three years, or you can drop your skill rating and push buttons. Welcome to Western." He licked his lips wolfishly.

So began another succession of days. Jason worked quickly through the assembly lines, more slowly in micro-circuitry. At home he studied, grudgingly doling credits for a leased scanner, until he was driven by loneliness to wander the malls of this new-old western city. Just under the two-month mark Monihan called him to the office again.

With a tinge of grumpy respect the manager walked Jason down the hall and into the design wing, showed him to a large cubicle and introduced him to several other men. "You'll do touch-ups on final-draft layouts to start," Monihan said. "Draughtsmanship never came easy. And never question a design." He stood in the doorway and threw a parting shot. "We should never have brought those robopicks in. Builds character to sweep up and empty baskets. See you in a year. Maybe." He whistled as he paced briskly up the hall.

Again it was a good bit less than that, for Jason stuck doggedly to his work and mastered it. He hadn't been concerned with draughtsmanship at Diamond Willow, but there was a peculiar satisfaction in producing perfect layouts; pulling scattered unit diagrams into a comprehensive, compact whole. He became more than efficient: he was first-rate. And he made friends. Some of the loneliness disappeared as he sat chatting in the autoteria over lunch or coffee. He joined the Men's Athletic Club, minutes from the Manor, played squash and basketball with his new friends. Even visited occasionally.

Perhaps it was their cramped standard ELS's that made him check one day, to learn with amazement how many credits he had on deposit. Or perhaps it was the people who eyed him distastefully in the lobby, sniffing at his plain swagger suit and conservative neckcloth. Mustering courage, he went shopping. He compromised not one whit once he had embarked on it, even though his tastes ran to a high credit range. He found that he enjoyed certain good wines, learning to choose them for particular dishes. And he nearly went on to the red when he slotted his AP Card for a complete multi-function homerec set. But it was worth it to have access to live music, cassettes, video, good books. Gone forever was the cheap scanner with its hookup to limited local microfiles. He had the resources of a continent at his fingertips.

The affected, oily manager stopped him in the lobby one evening, beaming with delight. "Mr. Berkley," he called, "I just wanted—that is—well." He cleared his throat. "When you first came you were, you know, painfully young and, er, crude. There were complaints from the other, uh, residents. I was on the verge of asking you to, ah, leave the Manor. To step down to a standard ELS someplace or, considering your credit rating, to move to one of the—Apartments—where you could be eccentric." Noting Jason's growing irritation, he forced a large, false smile. "What I'm trying to say is, it's so good to see you finally living up to your credits, Mr. Berkley," and with a nervous laugh he slithered away across the fluorescent blue carpet. Jason stood for a moment cooling down and then with a flash of insight he saw that the obnoxious manager was socially correct. More than that, he was correct for the Jason who was emerging more fully every day. His clothes, his pleasures were extensions of himself. That they met with social approval was convenient, but that they were naturally part of him was all-important.

Brusquely as ever, Monihan came for him one Friday in early summer and moved him again. "Re-opening an old line," he explained. "Computer blocks. Used to install them in multi-purpose remotes. The higher your clearance, the more blocks your key opened. Got too complicated," he added, "and they went to source blocks. Another company." He leaned back, fished out a cigar, and lit up. "Today, source blocks literally change a hundred times a day. Suppose you add a wrinkle: a micro-adjust key. Just before you use the remote, you match your key to a servo that adjusts it to everything in your clearance level." He looked quizzically at Jason, who said, "It should work. But then, computers aren't my special area." Monihan snorted. "Forget computers and think keys. Besides, you won't be doing the creative work. I have three other brains for that," he grunted. "You're going to review the old line and see how much of it you can shrink or discard, then pass on the essence."

So it went, and so it continued through the summer and on into the winter. He got similar jobs and stuck with each until he completed it to his own and Monihan's satisfaction. There were times when he pictured, in a flash of inspiration, the finished product which supposedly was far beyond his present abilities, but he remained observant and recognized with humility that the men above him arrived in their own ways at his conclusions. Sometimes they produced a better answer, though once or twice he knew that his design would be more effective. And it was while they were huddled over the final drawings of one such product that he met Ruth Hayworth.

Intent on schematics, he had become aware that the others were silent and over the end of the desk his glance dropped to a small, elegant sandal. It was like stop-action video: his gaze moved in jumps up the sheer, skin-tight aquapants, from trim calves to tapered thighs, to flaring hips; skittered over rounds of straining, translucent mesh, and was captured by a pair of amused, jade-green eyes. He stood up jerkily, reddening as he pushed down his rolled sleeves, knowing that she had already glimpsed the plate in his arm. Yet, aside from a warm, bright smile when they were introduced, Ruth had paid him no special attention. Instead, she unrolled the sheets of cover drawings she had brought and they had all gathered over the desk to admire the "finished" product. She was good, definitely. It was all exactly as the unit ought to look, yet somehow a little more impressive, more promising, displayed at just the right angle to flatter its lines. Jason joined in the general praise.

It was not, Jason realized later, accident that had brought her to his table in the autoteria a few weeks after. As before, her outfit was both daring and severe, revealing in contour, concealing in the appropriate places. It had the simplicity of elite credits. She was no older than he and still he stammered and moved clumsily, hating himself for his nervousness. Yet she seemed not to notice and after a while he had grown more assured. Lunch was over all too soon and he was back at work, bemused by it all and slow to think his way into the material in front of him. A few luncheons later he was amazed to hear himself suggest that they take in a wraparound. It had somehow, he also realized later, been the only time he was to suggest what they might do together.

Ruth Hayworth moved in a world which Jason had only dimly perceived. Far beyond the edge of his own interests. Now, nevertheless, he was slowly but surely drawn into it. "Pick me up at 19:00," she said. "We'll go to the big art bustout." And they went, mingling with the zany too-rich and noisily too-poor patrons and artists. Ruth introduced him to some, pointedly avoided others and carried on a constant chatter of criticism, background, information about the pieces, the people, the new movement. "You've got to hear the Troncon programme tonight," she told him, and he sat through an evening of devastating, ear-destroying symphony, listening as she explained the theory of sub- and supersonic underlay during intermission. Bit by bit, despite the hectic quality of their dates, a clear picture of the girl emerged. She was the daughter of a VP in Tundra Oil, an extremely high-credit man, and an indulgent mother who supplied anything she could put on the Family AP. With that, plus her own skill-credit rating, the girl lived as well as anyone could in a prairie province town. She had everything: talent, brains, beauty and credits; and she became intent upon using them all for Jason.

Not that she was the only woman in Jason's life. There was also Michelle Maigret—May-grey—as she tartly informed him the day they first crossed swords. She was, Jason supposed, one of the inconveniences of his creeping success at Western Safety. At twenty, he was now assigned by Monihan to a junior design engineer, at last allowed to work out the occasional innovation under the watchful eye of Stan Bolton. And Miss Maigret. Stan could have warned him, but it appeared that the older man was more than a little afraid of her himself. Jason had taken considerable trouble with his latest project, introducing a clever little scrambler circuit of which he was duly proud. Then, with no preamble, Michelle Maigret had stalked in, dropped the circuit drawing on his desk, X-ed a corner and said coldly, "Drop it."

It had not been exactly delicate, and he responded with vigour. She read him his lesson bluntly and dispassionately. "As cost analyst for this project, I say it goes. Oh, yes," she agreed, "it's beautiful. Ingenious. And it adds credits that push our sales extrapolations below margin." She won. She won several other arguments with Jason, but then no one could remember her ever having lost. It seemed incongruous that she, perhaps five years older than Jason, could thoroughly cow men twice her age, yet in her crisp, businesslike way she ticked off the hard facts and they wilted. Monihan was the only man to whom she showed deference and he treated her with a manner of near-equality.

Jason learned to accept her judgments and found, eventually, that she was rather attractive beneath the gruff exterior. He sensed that when she was particularly sharp with him she was using some sort of over-compensation and gradually he decided that she recognized a potential in him but that she was patterning herself somewhat after Monihan, who wouldn't be caught dead giving a compliment. Those deep brown eyes gave nothing away, the small, full body inclined not an iota further towards him, but there was that slight extra edge to her voice. He was, he reflected much later, still naive enough then to think he had figured it all out.

Meanwhile, his leisure time was more and more taken over by Ruth the energetic, Ruth the constant guide and mentor, who seemed never to tire of taking him to new, supposedly exotic places. She gave him her time, her knowledge, her friends and interests, and he marvelled at how selfless she was. She never allowed him to choose the places they went or to use his credits, never saw the inside of his ELS, though they spent hours in hers. It was as if she were determined to present him with a complete new life.

The culmination was, as such things so often are, a combination of sweet and bitter, of exultation and despair. In the crisp autumn air, touched with a trace of woodsmoke, they explored rocky little paths above the picturesque hunting lodge which her father seldom used. She delighted in showing him all the secret gadgets in and around the cabin, things which clashed with the raw majesty of the great silent peaks above them. Jason had felt his heart wrench at the first sight of those mountains, remembering his final rebellion in that other cabin far to the south. But he let Ruth go on, filled with the pleasure of giving, all through the short day and into the quick-dropping chill of twilight. Then, in the cheerful flicker of the great stone fireplace, she had given him the last thing of all. Slipping softly from his arms, she had stood before the fire, eyes glowing, full lips trembling and slowly loosened the belt of her long robe. She stood naked, breathtakingly beautiful in the golden light, and then came to him, arms open, heart pounding.

Jason had been surprised at the total assurance of his body, at the dual quality of participation and distant observation in his mind. It was manhood triumphant, and yet, in his absolute innocence, he knew that something was lacking. The woman who embraced him, enfolded him, was giving a great gift, but he, in return, was allowed to give nothing. Nothing but a brief spasm of his own future, doomed he was certain to quick extinction. In the fading light of the dying fire they lay together and she traced the letters of the plate in his arm with a fingertip so light that there was barely a tingle. "Poor Jason," she said. "The things they must have taken from you. I want so much to make it up." The words and their real meaning kept repeating in Jason's mind through the night, through their periods of desire and exhaustion. At base, though Ruth could never understand it, was a patronizing, selfish motive. If she weren't so thoroughly in love with life, Jason thought hollowly, she might have made a magnificent early martyr. A great, swollen red moon poured pale light into their bedroom and with sorrow as old as Adam's he stroked the sleeping girl's blonde hair, her face puffy with the satiation that comes of righteous giving.

The rest of their weekend was a mixture of impulsive sorties into the glorious colours of autumn and periods of passion in the artificially rustic cabin, but it was always the same. Jason became a practiced lover, still awed by the sexual responses of his body but chafed by the repetition of Ruth's giving without awareness of his isolation. At the centre of their relationship was an empty space and Jason intuitively grasped that it was an extension of the similar emptiness in Ruth's own life. They returned by roboflit on Monday evening, Jason still repelled by any suggestion of using the motorway, and he acknowledged a sense of relief.

Oh, they continued their intimacies. Well into the winter months they would end a frantic evening of "culture" twined in the age-old position, snug in the confines of Ruth's ELS. Yet Ruth herself slowly tired of the ritual and became a bit angry with herself when she dimly recognized that she could go no further with Jason. There was no more she could give now than what she had offered so unselfishly so many times. What else she expected she couldn't explain, but she saw that whatever it was would never come. Jason was tender, Jason was grateful, but Jason was still—Jason. By January they were meeting less often, by February not at all. There was no scene, no formal parting, only a drawing apart till they smiled and talked vacantly when they shared a table in the autoteria.

Jason sorted out and made part of his character the intangible things he learned from it. There were now, however, other problems which kept him occupied. He was still assistant to Stan Bolton, though he knew he had in fact outgrown the job. Bolton was affable, but there was a tension in the man that belied his surface assurance. Strangely enough, it was not during the nerve-wracking initial stages of a project that he tightened up. It was after the breakthrough that Stan ("Call me Stan, Jase," he said heartily) became jumpy, almost secretive. Jason had discounted his suspicions until he could no longer thrust away what was clearly evident. Bolton was working at his absolute limit. He would never be more than a junior engineer, was perhaps not suited for that level, since one cannot keep working indefinitely at one's limit. Yet he survived and how he did it was beyond Jason. Until the day in early March when Jason got the answer.

They had grappled for weeks with a tricky little problem, an elusive matter of placing an unshielded modulator amid raucous, indiscriminate circuits crammed into a ring face. Diplomatic Corps. Designed to open locks that supposedly didn't exist. So said Monihan, who thus obliquely informed Jason that at least his security clearance had gone up. It had really been his baby, as the micro-circuit specialist, and he had stayed long nights alone with Stan, seeking the solution. When it came it was perversely simple. A red-eyed Jason, rubbing the sweaty stubble on his jaw, had wandered home cursing himself for not seeing the answer long before, though in the morning he gained a just pride in the completed diagram.

Some days later Monihan appeared in the doorway, Michelle Maigret behind him, and held up the binder. "Great job, Stan," he said with rare praise. "You've got a classic here. Should be good for a few juicy contracts." He placed a hand on Stan's shoulder and added, "Especially that modulator chamber. A stroke of genuine genius." Jason had looked up, expectant. Stan had flushed uncomfortably, muttered something trivial like "Always willing to please," and launched into speculation about the present project. He looked at Monihan and Michelle, at sketches, anywhere but at Jason, who sat with a cold feeling growing in the pit of his stomach. He sat, and realized that Stan was waiting in agony for him to claim his due. To Jason's acute eye, the junior engineer was so wound up that his reaction would be totally unpredictable and with mixed feelings of disgust and self-recrimination he held his tongue.

What to do about it? He knew now why he was still assistant to Stan. Over the next few days and nights he puzzled it over, seizing and discarding notion after notion. From sick disgust he swung to savage anger, then to weak helplessness. He didn't know what might happen when he and Stan came face to face, but Stan, with guilty cunning, avoided the confrontation. He took a combined holiday and tour of parts plants to the south, leaving abruptly with his family and with Monihan's blessing. Jason, in the meantime, remained to do a mass of routine items, circle round and round his problem and end without a definite course of action.

Fortunately, it was during this time of torment that Michelle Maigret slipped casually, informally into his life. As Ruth had done, ages ago it seemed, she sat with him one day in the autoteria and they chatted over lunch. She had begun with a trifle of shop talk and then quite deliberately dropped it. Speaking of other things, politics, books, people, she had become warm and animated, creating an illusion of decreasing stature, shrinking authority. No! That was wrong, Jason decided after their third or fourth meeting. The illusion was that of the stern, formidable woman of statistics and efficiency, a cultivated posture calculated to ensure acceptance in a largely male environment. At twenty-six or seven she had made herself as indispensable as anyone could be in this society, where jobs for skill-ratings were all too scarce and mindless button-pushers abounded. Michelle was clearly, very clearly, an intelligent and vital human being, with her own special desires and needs.

April first had nearly passed when Jason, struck by the date on a scanner memo, tidied up his desk a few minutes early and on rash impulse stuck his head in at her door. "It's my birthday, Michelle," he explained. "Would you like to help me celebrate?" He felt awkward as he had not been in years, but she smiled and said with genuine pleasure, "Why I'd love to."

There was one restaurant where Jason had spent pleasant evenings alone, lingering over the luxury of good food, good surroundings and good service. He and Michelle sat long after they had finished eating, free of frenzied Musak or impatient queues. In the real candlelight her eyes were huge and dark, the small face like cool ivory against the background of lush tapestries. Jason had the strange sensation that his very spirit was expanding as they talked. Nothing of consequence was said, but yet it was deeply significant that he spoke of things he had painfully reasoned out, that she accepted them, matched them with her own, and they traded private things, the dreams which were themselves.

On the fragile span of the high-level walkway they paused, silent, and looked far down into the distant cacophony of the city, all the way to the rushing, disquieting blur of light ribboning the motorway and Jason turned and gently drew up the tall stylish collar of her cloak, hiding the tiny ears and short black hair. At twenty-one, he was beginning to grasp the true meaning of an old phrase: "Peace within us."

They lay lazily in an alder-fringed recess on the bluff of the North Saskatchewan, welcoming the uncommon heat of a June day and looked across the alluvial beige of the swift river, the rich brown ploughed land, towards the hazy outline of the city. This was the first time that she had suggested a place and she had offered it shyly, partly because she didn't want to impose and partly, he understood, because it was a special private place which she had found. The path had been indistinguishable from below and as they stood breathless on the summit she had waited in girlish embarrassment for his approval. Then they had settled to talk, chins propped on hands, stretch-ed out on his huge, shaggy blanket in the comfort of one another's company.

Later they were quiet, pensive, and Michelle turned to gaze into Jason's eyes. Still without speaking she pushed herself up and knelt, taking his hand in both of hers. He rolled on to his knees and cupped his free hand behind her head, drawing her forward to kiss her tender-ly, then with increasing strength and quickening breath. She raised his hand in hers to her throat, held it there between her palms almost in an attitude of prayer and then dropped her arms to her sides. As if entranced, he slowly slipped the seal of her tunic downward, all the way to the hem and the short garment parted slightly. He kissed her again, a long reassuring touch, and softly put his hands on her shoul-ders, pushing the tunic out and back, down her arms and away. Through the new leaves of the alders, dappled sunlight wove a soft pattern across her small, full breasts, and he bent to rest his cheek against them as she sank slowly back on to the blanket. She lay be-side him barely moving, throat pulsing, gazing mutely as he traced the line of her curving hip, sliding filmy cloth under his hand. And at last, with a breaking storm of passion she drew him to her, crying out gently in her need.

They shared. They shared their need, their giving, the secrets of body and soul. And within Jason something came together with an all-but-audible sound. He was whole, complete at last, but aware as never before of his humanity, of Michelle's wonderful vulnerable humanity. He could never again deliberately isolate himself, for though he had mastered himself he understood the utter need of one human being for another.

"Jase," Michelle murmured later, "thank you. Thank you for being you, and helping me to be myself." And she hugged him fiercely amid mixed laughter and tears.

● ● ● ● ●

Dependence—Independence. Later in the night, back in his ELS, he weighed the two and absorbed the fact that too few people ever learn. You can't have one without the other, he concluded, as he padded restlessly through the cramped space. Funny, but now he could search his thoughts and find no animosity for Stan Bolton, only sadness. It wasn't a matter of his own wrongs any more. What concerned him was a feeling of frustration that there was no way to help the older man. Stan was trapped in a strange way, not simply by a job that demanded too much, but by the inability to rid himself of guilt. Jason had let it pass, and now there was nothing that he could do to help. Perhaps Stan had been beyond that before they met, but Jason would have given the world to be able to do something for him.

It was strange, too, that within days of the miraculous afternoon with Michelle, Monihan had called him to his office, silently handing him a priority cassette and motioning him to the scanner at his desk. Jason had read with shocked disbelief, looking up to find Monihan watching him with haunted eyes.

"You know?" Jason asked.

"I can guess," Monihan answered, rubbing his arm with a peculiar gesture. "You've been ordered back to Diamond Willow." Jason nodded, pondering the curt message that told him simply to pack, terminate present affairs and report this same evening.

The manager crossed to him and clasped his hand. "You've come a long way in three years," he said. "We've watched you develop and you've got the rare quality to make it to the top. Things like the ring face modulator." A bitter smile flickered at his lips and was gone, as Jason started. "We want you," he said firmly. "Remember that." He took Jason's elbow and led him to the door. "Now say your good-byes, and get the blazes out of here." The door closed hard as Jason moved off down the hall.

Michelle made it easier than he had expected and he calmly added the fact that she already knew to those other bits that were coming together. Monihan was a wise, observant man, all in all. But she also made it clear that what was between them, the supple bond of sharing and understanding, had nothing whatsoever to do with the manager. For observer, he was, not manipulator. Everything Jason had gained was completely of his own fashioning.

"I'm going to Montreal soon," Michelle said. "Not everyone in this organization is bilingual." She smiled and gave him a long kiss, held him around the waist and leaned back to look at him. "Scribe the odd line? No cassettes. And life is a lot longer than we think." Their fare-well was neutral, neither final nor promising.

He stood in the same indoctrination chamber again and this time the three men were positively ageing. The first addressed him in a flat, dispassionate voice. "Jason Berkley, you have now reached the end of Phase Two. You have become capable of understanding the nature of your offence and the memory blocks will be removed, after which you will receive your sentence." Jason was staggered by the massive surprise of it. Sentence? He had somehow thought that the time in school . . . But as he groped for stability his arm tingled, a sharp finger of pain jerked his head upright and with appalling clarity a sequence of memory lay stark before him.

He was standing on a ramp, a construction ramp, over the motorway, cutters in hand and a coil of cable weighing down his shoulder, listening. The roar of the motorway was insistent, drawing and repelling him at once and slowly it pulled him nearer to the edge, till the racing vehicles thirty metres below seemed to merge into a double ribbon of blurred motion. The cutters dropped from his hand and a swelling wave of blind hatred welled up in him and spilled over, spilled over as a coil of cable snaking crazily into the maw of sound. Above the steady roar there was a grinding shriek and one vehicle rose from the line, cartwheeled through the air and slammed into the concrete bank beyond the service lane. A form lay twisted half out of one window, another crumpled in a shapeless mass metres away and from beneath the wreckage crawled a tiny figure, clothes torn, streaming blood, to sit with mouth gaping in a soundless scream.

Jason was sent reeling by the horror of what he had seen, aghast at the inexorable conviction that he must have, he had, done this. The image of the child burned its way into his mind until, with another sharp pang, he *was* the child. No! Another child, older, in an earlier time, sobbing at the emergency exit of a motorway, looking back at the fiery inferno that enclosed—who? Vague faces with indistinct features. Father! Mother! And sister, or was it brother? Baby! And himself, six or seven, scrabbling and shrieking into the sub-levels, coiling into a foetal ball for an interminable time, to wander later through myriad passages, shrinking back from any human voice, living off the droppings from servoscoffers.

He came back to the present shuddering, beyond control of his revolted body, to hear the second man speak. "You know the circumstances now," he said in a dead voice. "The law must be satisfied." And he nodded towards the first man. "But your action had its root causes and, further, society has uses for your abilities. You have demonstrated your value." The third man continued in a voice softer than Jason had ever heard any of them use. "Jason, the law must be upheld, the society will have its ultimate gram of productivity." He acknowledged the other two with a hard glance. "Justice, however, is for the individual first, the law and society second. Let the punishment fit the man, or boy if you wish, and not his crime." A touch of sadness entered his voice. "You have become a man now, in a depth greater than most achieve. You have need to expiate, knowing the full extent of your guilt. Justice will provide you the means."

He sat back with an air of infinite weariness and finished. "You will proceed to room 220, MacKenzie Wing, for orientation to Phase Three." The cubicle went dead and Jason left the chamber, leaning dizzily against the wall for a moment as he tried desperately to keep his balance, physical and mental. He noted, finally, that his arm was tingling and pushed up his sleeve weakly, to read the new shimmering word—*Interdependence.*

The boy was poised in a half-crouch, a few feet into the great hall, eyes flicking from robocop at the double doors to the young man in the black utility suit. Teeth bared in a snarl, shaved skull gleaming, he looked like some trapped animal hurling defiance at his captors. The grey eyes hooded as he spied the smaller door at the side of the hall and with a feint towards the robocop he uncoiled into a sprint, only to crumple in mid-air and spill to a helpless sprawl, gazing up at the fuzzy figure in black that towered over him. As strength oozed back into arms and legs, he saw clearly, and the young man gently, quietly, reached down and lifted him to his feet.

"Peace," Jason said to him, in a voice filled with compassion. "Peace and unity within these walls, and within ourselves."

5 5 5

n Man eV

5

Tee Vee Man

5

William E. Baldwin, technician, sat cross-legged on his bunk, doggedly chewing the end of a pencil. Wedged between his knees was a clipboard holding a paper covered with neat columns of figures. A passing crewman might have supposed that he was working out the formula for a world-shaking discovery. "Two hundred," he muttered. "Two hundred and two, specifically, for roofing and chimney repairs, paint, and new fencing. Dammit, even on risk pay we never get ahead."

As he looked away from the unchanging figures, Baldwin glanced at the bulkhead beside him. A trio of smiling faces looked back at him, seeming full of pride for their spaceman hero. "Hero," he bit out grimly. Little did his wife and children know of his true position on the space platform. With sudden bitterness, Baldwin slammed the clipboard into his tiny locker and stretched out tensely, hands behind his head. On this unique platform, this little flyspeck, were thirty-five of the best brains that Earth had produced. Thirty-five genii, gathered from nearly as many countries—and Baldwin, employee of International Communications: Baldwin, the Tee Vee man. His mouth tightened as he sub-voiced the words.

Tee Vee man. It didn't seem to matter that only three of the twenty-seven satellites he serviced were television relays, that the rest were vital navigation, weather, and surveillance satellites. To the indifferent thinking-machines around him he was the TV technician, a target for superior smiles, a body grudgingly given much-needed space, food, and air. These men, designers of most of their own jealously-guarded equipment, would have thrown a fit if a mere engineer so much as peeped into their private work areas, much less traced a circuit. He was unwanted there, and virtually ignored elsewhere when he chanced on conversations involving anything from space medicine to astro-physics. Perhaps it might have been different if he had gone on past his Master's, put off marriage a little longer, even turned down the job offered to him by the hybrid giant that had eventually sent him out here.

The glory of research and design had worn off when he found that international politics could reach into the depths of his lab, but he had not learned the full lesson. It had remained for him to be wooed into space training, to arrive on the space-platform and find himself considered hired help. Only then could he realize that he was caught between two worlds; in the one a professional who knew too little of business and politics, in the other a hireling of business and politics who knew too little of the professions surrounding him. In neither world, it seemed, was he judged as an individual, by merits that had weight in normal situations.

"At any rate," he growled, "in two months my tour is over. One more after that, and back to solid ground for good. But not back to I.C. Back to school." On that thought, and the probability that he would have to move his family again, Baldwin reached for the clip-board, hoping to work a little magic on the cold figures.

"Baldwin . . . Baldwin . . . Communications."

He dropped into the narrow aisle, stepped to the hatch, lifted a phone and thumbed a button. "Communications . . . Baldwin."

"A wee job for you, Tee Vee," said the dry voice of MacPherson, mathematician. "One of your yo-yos, TV 2, is out of service. Terrible fuss from downstairs, and you're to get on it, as of now. I've run a tape into your bronco, and you've five minutes minus twenty to most favourable position. You go down the North Pole chute this time, and just so you won't buzz your old folks in Canada I've plotted the whole course. Don't get lost, man, the set in the lounge is actin' up."

"Right," snapped Baldwin, and moved off through the passage toward the Hub and the airlock. He cursed mildly to himself. It would have to be a TV satellite. Probably it had been Melling who sent the message. To him everything was an emergency, since he was obviously uncertain of his future in the company. A holdover from the original, he was in danger of replacement by Zoldovski, his counterpart in the "other" original, and half the time his budget was held up by the Red Asia bloc.

Reaching the airlock, Baldwin suited up, then dropped the air pressure and checked out. Everything working fine, as usual, he thought, and as he flexed the pliothene gloves he added aloud, "Probably still too much heat dissipation." Well, he'd had a touch of frostbite every time out. He pumped the remaining air back into the tanks, opened the outer hatch, and dove across to the bronco. He slipped the single mooring cable and closed the hatch, then settled into the huge seat and hooked up his suit connections. "Communications . . . Baldwin. Radio check."

"Five by five," answered MacPherson. "Your red light shows in ninety-three minutes thirty, so you've not much time to do the job. Up at the South Pole, laddie, and don't be late, as we've a one-shot sighting to take. Besides, your Mister Melling says it's vital to have the African network back in the grid within two hours. Twenty-two seconds, Baldwin. Don't catch cold out there."

Baldwin fumed as the webbing closed around him. The Scotsman seemed to be rubbing it in, as usual. He could just as well have homed on TV 2 and not taken any more time, once he got below the Van Allen Belt. Then, suddenly, he was shoved back into the seat as the bronco took off at maximum gees. For a wild second he considered strangling the Scotsman. "Full acceleration, and then full deceleration," he groaned. A very poor joke, or a nasty way to show him his place. Whichever it was, he would have a talk with MacPherson when he got back. Then, as acceleration lifted, he turned to the job ahead.

MacPherson had mentioned the African network—it would have to be that area to cause such a furor. If only the satellites had come a little later the dark continent might have had cable or microwave connections to the world grid, to serve in just such emergencies as this. Then there wouldn't be a scream of anguish every time some South African housewife missed The Internation Cookbook. As the bronco's verniers spat briefly, bringing it under the Belt and down in a sweeping arc across Labrador and Newfoundland, Baldwin twisted and looked up at Earth, to spot the dawn band lying full across the eastern Atlantic. New curses rattled behind his teeth as he estimated it to be about 10:00 A.M., in Algiers. Then his head snapped forward as deceleration began, and his temper neared the boiling point.

Below TV 2, at a remote spot in Central Africa, the capital city of a small, newly-independent country was nearing its boiling point too. A mass of contradictions, the city of some fifty thousand was a place where anything might happen, and something quite ugly could happen on this particular day. Anyone approaching Ungalah on the ground, along every road including that from the country's one airport, would have been struck by large groups of semi-permanent huts, each housing a few members of a different tribe. Their pointed roofs echoed the lines of a single, great ultra-modern building soaring above and beyond them, at the centre of the city.

At the edge of the city proper wretched, ramshackle quarters of all descriptions huddled and leaned against one another, giving way only a few streets from the huge central square to old shops, then modern, spacious stores. Late-model vehicles mingled with wood-burning buses and oxcarts; neat-suited businessmen and government officials with tribesmen in local costume. Normally the babble, screech and clamour would have been deafening, but today there was an uneasy quiet over most of the city. Only in the square facing the government building was there any sound, any real sense of life. Here four thousand tribes-men from the northern province sat, squatted, and stood, body to body, murmuring among themselves, gesturing toward the end of the square. The assortment of arms among them, carried in open defiance of the law, was antique by modern standards, but nonetheless deadly. That these men and their weapons were a force to be reckoned with could be judged by the numbers of nervous troops ranked in front of the great building, ranged down its flanks, and scattered through the lobbies.

It was neither the tribesmen nor the troops facing them, however, that commanded immediate attention at the moment. Rather, it was a strange device raised precisely at the top of the broad steps leading up to the buildings. Fully twenty feet high and thirty long, it had a vast hood extending out from its top and down its sides. Even as the tribesmen were becoming dangerously restive there came a crackling, a sudden whine which slowly died away, and a figure appeared on what now could be identified as a TV extension screen.

As the screen brightened, this figure became recognizable, and though none of them had ever been in to the building behind the screen it was obvious to the watchers that he was seated in a room somewhere in that building. A bellow of disapproval rose, and one giant of a man, clad in little more than a massive headdress, waved an ancient sword as he pushed toward the screen through the milling mob. Then as the figure spoke the din slowly settled into silence.

"My friends from the north," the seated man said in grave tones, "it would give me great pleasure to welcome you to the capitol on any occasion, if you had come in peace. Indeed, although I am leader of the opposition party, and the prime minister is of your venerable tribe, you have been most hospitable to me on my visits to your villages. Your response to me when I have spoken to you on the great picture makers in your own province has always been courteous too, so I am told, though you seem not to choose my vote tokens at elections."

Here he smiled tensely, and a wave of ironic comment swept the square. At the far end an old, bent and scarred veteran shouted a rude suggestion about the tokens and the young men gathered around him, lifted him high in the air so he could repeat it. In his office on the top floor, the seated man turned from the cameras and stole a glance out the window at his side, down into the square, to see a ripple of movement spread from the old man like waves from a dropped pebble. He wiped his palms on his trousers, under the desk, and continued.

"I can understand your mood today. You want to see your leader. There are certain people who would like you to think that he is in some sort of danger. They have told you that he has come to harm, that we of the opposition have taken him away, that we have dealt with him as other leaders, in other times, have been dealt with." A hint of revulsion passed across his face briefly, as below the giant waved his sword again and screamed at the screen, drawing a hideous response from the tribesmen behind him. "First let me say," the voice boomed over them, "that those times are gone. As many things have passed away and new things have taken their places in our lives, so new ideas have come to us, new ways of handling the problems of leadership, new ways of settling differences of opinion. I, Albert N'Galy, swear to you that your leader is safe."

In the pause that followed, men looked to the old veteran, now standing on a stone bench, and to the giant, who suddenly found himself almost under the screen, yards in front of the rest. The old man, conscious of his growing power, once again hurled abuse down the square toward the distant screen, while the giant, uncomfortably close to the troops, turned and voiced his rage to the crowd in incoherent shouts, punctuated by thrusts of his sword.

One, two, five minutes went by as the tumult reached its climax and subsided, while in his office the speaker waited and watched, sweat soaking into his shirt and jacket. Choosing his time carefully, he spoke forcefully but without shouting into his microphone, overriding the dying roar.

"Your leader is safe, I repeat. Although he is many miles away, across the sea, Nicolas N'Thulmah is quite safe. Indeed, he is acting for all of us to receive an honour which we must find almost impossible to conceive. At this very moment he is in the company of the head men of all the great countries of the world: he, our leader, is to speak before them, to carry our thanks for being welcomed into the great assembly of chiefs, United Nations. It is a time of which we should all be proud, not a time to behave like animals."

In the square, the giant was silent as he tried to digest and assess this new information. Behind him muttering began, swelling slowly into a roar, and the old man cried, "It's a trick. Show us N'Thulmah. Show us Nicolas the Beloved."

The figure on the screen stood up, held out its hands. One more time, desperately aware of the scene below him, N'Galy was able to subdue the mob. "Many of you have seen on the picture makers people moving within United Nations on important occasions. It has been arranged that we should see Nicolas N'Thulmah welcomed, as our leader, to the great hall of chiefs. If you see him there, will you believe he is all right?"

The old man pondered this for a moment, as a small buzz of consultations went round and slowly grew into a confused sound of assent. Sensing the mood of those around him, the old man held his silence, content to wait for the right time. The figure on the screen sat down again, and his face grew until it filled the screen. The onlookers could see lines of strain, the look of anxiety, as he stared straight out into the mob.

"Then you must be patient a little longer," he said. "It is only a matter of a little time. There are some problems with the picture maker's workers. They cannot make the picture come across the ocean yet. But it will not be long." His voice increased in volume toward the end of this statement, as he anticipated the reaction below, and it was immediate in coming.

The giant was shouting again, moving toward the base of the screen, and the tribesmen surged toward him. At the rear, the veteran began a chant and his young followers joined him, spreading it until the whole far end of the square resounded with the one word: "Now . . . Now!" On the top floor, N'Galy nodded toward his office door and an officer moved to the elevator. Below him, harried non-coms moved back and forth, out of sight, cautioning, checking, encouraging their men as the sounds of frustration and disapproval rolled over them.

Frustration and disapproval were still with William Baldwin too, as the bronco homed in on TV 2 and automatically matched course and velocity, with a precision that worked to less than one kph and a thousandth of a degree. He turned on his floods and watched as the turning satellite seemed to move in and up on his starboard side, an inch at a time, until it blocked out the blackness of space. At last all relative movement ceased. He saw the last green light come on, turned his suit on to self-function and disengaged it, locked the propulsion panel, and extended his work shield in a semi-circle around TV 2. One more careful check of the control panels and he climbed out the hatch and along the flooring of his shield.

A fantastic amount of knowledge, some of it gained from painful experience, had gone into the design of this part of the bronco. Here, mounted or stowed in the shield itself, were tools, meters, spare gates and rods, an auxiliary control panel, the visuo-library index for securing all information concerning the satellites under his care. Some things he had installed himself, just as a large amount of the design in the satellites had been modified, on his insistence, to facilitate maintenance aloft. In the old days, before the platform, a satellite had either worked or been replaced, but when it became economical to service them in orbit, sweeping changes had occurred. Even when Baldwin had no inkling that he would become an early "repairman" he had put nearly all of his time into standardization of design and simplification of access. It had already payed off a thousandfold.

TV 2, antennae automatically retracted by gyroscopic equipment apparently still functioning perfectly, turned on its axis with a deceptively lazy motion that was still too fast for a visual check. Baldwin carefully extended booms, snapped them to the eyebolts mounted on the satellite's axis, and fastened his lifeline. Diving out to the end of one boom, he snapped a switch in the eyebolt and kicked off back to the shield. He brought slight pressure onto the booms and watched the great satellite slow to a stop, moving it in close with the damaged area facing him. Something had holed the skin, peeling it back over a two-foot gash between the points of entry and exit.

He glanced at a meter in the shield, knowing that it would show a reduced internal temperature, but though it was dropping visually, it was still not as bad as he had expected. Working sunside would make it easier anyway, he thought, and started the Jesperson equalizer. Heat bathed the area as the collectors on the front of his shield began to function and the dissipators spread it around TV 2.

He pulled a cutting torch from its holder and methodically cut away the jagged pieces of fuselage, placing them on the flooring where they clung lightly. This was the simplest part of the job, and as he worked he allowed his mind to return to MacPherson and his colleagues. He knew that none of them realized how intricate or dangerous this work could be. The library was a cute gadget, but actually the technician relied mainly on a crammed memory, ingenuity, and sometimes inspiration. There simply wasn't enough time to do much rehashing at orbit, and if he did pull one and haul it back he had lots of time for review at the platform, though he'd have to sabotage his radio to keep off the abuse from below.

The impact area was cleared now, and he turned back to the job at hand, checking the large chronometer face near the top of the work shield. Twenty-eight minutes to red light. He concentrated on the satellite. "Number three power supply, all units," he grunted, as he pried at the fused mass. It had thrown a little radiation around too, but not into any vital sections. He flexed his suit gloves thoughtfully and dug deeper into the guts of the satellite. Have to swing one gate at least, he mused, and reached for the magnakey. With both feet planted, and one hand on the satellite, he placed the key over a slug with great precision. Pressing the stud, he activated the magnet and felt the slug move up and out. A half-turn locked it in the out position and he moved to the next.

Six slugs later he was looking at the rest of the damage. Two rods of video useless, all of the power supply, a section of hi-voltage cable, and probably one more rod, to be sure. Quickly, almost mechanically, he extracted the wrecked components, not bothering to replace anything individual. Like pulling hen's teeth, he winced, as tiny prongs twisted and broke in their sockets and he went after them one by one. He took two adjacent rods as an added precaution and spares for these went into place easily. Eighteen minutes to red light.

He wired in the hi-voltage-cable with a spot welder. Next the video units went in. One of them went hard, but he got it into place and it checked out. Last the power supply had to be eased in. He even smiled slightly as he hefted the one hundred odd pounds of ultra-light miracle, thinking of what a job it would have been to handle it on earth. All connectors in place, he moved to his bank of meters and remote adjustment equipment. Fingers moving quickly, he set dials, snapped switches, watched a tiny monitoring screen. The antennae slid partway out, just clearing the shield. Power on. A high reading in the video stages . . . damped. On the screen a blurred scene began to appear. He made more adjustments from the panel, and noted the results as they were completed within the satellite. The picture was clearing. Too late he realized that TV 2 was swinging in behind him, that the booms had somehow become unlocked.

As he reached wildly for the boom controls, the bulk of the satellite touched his leg, pressing it against the pile of fuselage fragments. Pain shot through his body, blinding him, threatening to black him out, and then it was over. The huge mass swung slowly, idly backward. It had been a light brush, not enough to crush his leg, but it had been enough. Fighting off terror, he looked down at his suit. Only a thin line appeared to tell him that a fragment had sliced through the self-sealing unit, and his dial told him that there was no leak. But inside the suit something far more serious had happened. He could feel a jet of warm fluid splashing against his leg, feel the warmth of his own blood seeping down around his ankle, into the boot of the suit. Panic rose in him again as he knew that an artery was severed in the calf of his leg.

Struggling to remain calm he dove across the flooring and whipped out a piece of spare cable. In near hysteria he wrapped it tightly around his leg, a little below the knee. He fumbled with it, managed a clumsy knot, stuck a screwdriver through it, and twisted. The pain became intense, but he felt the pulsing jet slow and seem to stop. No time to judge whether it would hold against suit pressure, or what it would do to air circulation. He shot a glance at the chronometer as he cleared the shield flooring and flipped off switches. Seven minutes to red light.

He grabbed a large piece of patch metal, much too large for the job, but there was no time to cut it now. The satellite was too far out now. Swing the booms—lock them this time. Working frantically he tacked corners and ran a rough weld down the edges. No time to make a further check, no time to lock the gate, the welded section would have to hold it. Dizziness was mounting in him as he moved hand-over-hand to the end of the boom and snapped the eyebolt switch. He dove back to the shield as TV 2 began to spin again. Hit the boom release, climb back through the hatch. As he passed the monitoring screen he could see a black figure, mouth working silently. His last thought as he fell into the seat and wiped his hand across the propulsion panel and shield retractor switches was that he had never checked the audio. Then, as the red light went on and webbing closed around him, acceleration crushed him back into the seat and on into oblivion.

In the city of Ungalah, bolts snicked back on weapons as the troops straightened their ranks to face four thousand surging tribesmen. Far down the square, the old man, carried on eager young shoulders, urged the crowd to vengeance, and at the very top of the steps the giant, all feelings banished now save the lust of battle, waved his sword and screamed a war cry. Muzzles came up as the mob hit the first step behind him, heads turned slightly toward officers whose arms were upraised to give the signal. Then, suddenly, a new cry rose in the square.

From back to front it swept the ranks of tribesmen and all movement stopped. Every eye turned toward the screen as the face of Nicolas N'Thulmah swam up out of greyness. The view changed slightly and behind him the background of the United Nations Assembly Hall appeared. Abruptly the liquid, smooth voice of their leader filled the air. His language was strange, but it was clearly his voice. Then it was replaced by one speaking in their own tongue, their own dialect.

"Many of you here," it said, "have become accustomed to the welcoming of a new nation to your ranks. A few, more recent members, will understand, will recall, the emotions that fill me as I accept, for my people, a place among the nations of the world."

The rest was lost as a thunder of triumph rattled the windows of the government building, and swords and spears waved a fierce greeting to the leader. The sound seemed almost to shake Albert N'Galy down further into his seat, but as he tilted back his head and closed his eyes he smiled weakly.

Back aboard the space platform, William Baldwin reclined, if one could call it that, in the narrow confines of his bunk. He grimaced distastefully at the bottle hanging from the bunk close above his head, and the tube leading to his arm. Slowly, painfully, he raised himself slightly and looked down the length of his body. His blanket was pinned securely. Well, he thought, doctors are the same anywhere, whether they're space researchers or horse doctors. From the feel of it they put ten pounds of dressing on my leg. I'd probably be better off with a horse doctor or a good G.P.

He settled back again and wondered what would happen now. Would they send up a special replacement for him? Melling would have a fit if that were necessary . . . it would take pretty near the whole U.N. portion of the budget for a year to do that. But then, he mused, someone will have to go under and finish the job on TV 2: it can't be a first-class performer with that patchwork. But why should it be Baldwin who risked his neck again, why shouldn't it be some other sucker sent up to take over this thankless grind, someone with a thicker skin? Then, despite himself, he grinned. That could be taken as a rotten pun. He winced with pain again as he turned on his side to see who had come through the hatch, and felt a stirring of the anger as MacPherson came alongside his bunk.

"Well," frowned the balding Scotsman, "loafing on the company's time I see, eh Baldwin?" The injured man felt his face flush, and he pushed up slightly to throw a hot reply back, but the Scotsman went blithely on. "I've a wee communication from your Mister Melling for a change. He says you're to take as long as you need to recover, but he would like you to touch up TV 2 in a couple of days. Seems it's a mite wobbly on its axis, and the audio fades."

Baldwin fell back on to his pillow. No reprieve, he thought. I should tell him to go to . . .

"Oh yes," continued MacPherson, "there was somethin' else too." He glanced at a flimsy in one hand. "The U.N. sends its appreciation for your prompt action during crisis. You, uh, removed the possibility of a bloody insurrection in some unpronounceable African state or other." He rolled the words with an exaggerated burr, and for the first time that Baldwin could remember the dour Scotsman smiled. "And we thought the occasion demanded some little token, since you won't be able to go down in person for some time yet. This is from all of us." His face grew serious again as he brought his other hand from behind his back. Between thumb and forefinger dangled a ribbon, obviously cut from someone's underwear, and from it was suspended a gigantic, star-shaped piece of metal. Scratched into it in bold letters was the word, "Hero".

MacPherson turned to leave. "The butcher-boys say you can hobble in three days, and get back to work in a week, but they're like all the male midwives down below. Just between us, can you kind of rush it? The set in the lounge is gettin' really bad now, and we need a Tee Vee man." He popped back through the hatch, whistling, as Baldwin lay back and held up his medal.

6

More Things in Heaven and Earth

6

There are more things in heaven and earth,
  Horatio,
Than are dreamt of in your philosophy.

                                    Hamlet

●

He woke, as always, easily and instantly alert, feeling a well-being that brought him off the bed with lithe grace, facing the curtained window wall. Thumbing the switch at the end of a long, slow stretch, he watched as the curtains parted and slid into their receptacles, revealing a sweeping view of the Great Plains. He stepped forward and touched the faintly visible seam of the window, then breathed deeply as he moved through the opening on to his balcony. Before him was an unbroken mass of protected parkland; off to the extreme right the perimeter of that imposing complex of modern architecture—University Television Central. Consciously appreciating the day, he went through the routine of setting-up exercises, allowing his body to savour the sensuous pleasure of hard work. That done, he stripped off his sleepsuit, showered and dressed, dialled breakfast and a newsfax, retrieved his All Purpose Card, and reviewed the schedule for the day.

   Alan Hamilton, senior lecturer, accepted his position of eminence in the academic world much as he had every other upward step in his career; neither with smugness nor humility, but the simple and complete satisfaction of knowing that he was where he best fitted at his stage of development. He knew vaguely that he was envied by many people, even disliked or misunderstood by some of his lesser colleagues, but he was thoroughly engrossed by the work he did superlatively well. On the rare occasion when he was forced to comment on his success, he gave a large measure of the credit, and quite properly, to The Unit, the group of talented people whom he had painstakingly assembled around him, and who were essential to the preparation of his course material. They too were the envy of the whole profession, and their unique fusion as a production team sometimes prompted less talented people to hint at a dark, and totally fictitious, incestuous relationship within the group.

He was, however, unconscious of one fact: that it was an element of his own personality which was largely responsible for the cohesion of The Unit, and its ease of making tangible the complex interpretations which he derived from the plays of Shakespeare. This was the same element which enabled him to communicate so readily by means of television ideas which clearly, in written form, had fewer dimensions than those projected to his students spread through the mid-third of the continent. Projection was probably the word which defined that element best; a rare gift that only the truly great teachers and performers have possessed.

Breakfast finished, and the news as boringly full of discontent and clashes as always, Hamilton decided to skip the pedexpress, and instead chose the high-level walkway, where he could still enjoy the fine weather and mull over some tenuous thoughts about the day's lecture on *Richard III.* There were one or two minor suggestions that he would make to The Unit, possibilities which they hadn't covered in the previous two days of discussion, experimentation, and rehearsal. There was, for example, a slight change of inflection in Richard's "As I am subtle, false, and treacherous" which could better de-emphasize the modern psychological interpretation of Richard. He would call it to Ben Bowman's attention. Ben would like it, being more inclined to the Machiavellian interpretation—not that he gave any less effort to the psychological when it was required, as it invariably was by the students. One by one, he clarified his ideas until he arrived below the peak of BC, the broadcast control tower which had been intended as *avant garde* but had somehow wound up looking like a reconstructed pyramid.

Once inside the buildings, Hamilton moved swiftly through the maze of corridors, plummeted into the depths on an express elevator, and turned in at the broadcast production area. Mind still on his lecture, he was startled when, from the open door next to his own, a deep voice called, "Alan! Can you spare a moment?" Sam Meynard, executive producer of the Shakespeare course, half-rose from his desk and motioned. "I know it's a damned imposition so close to lecture time," he rumbled, "but someone upstairs has a real squeeze on this time. Sit down for just a second and I'll give you the score." Alan propped restlessly against a low file deck, and Sam rapidly filled in the problem.

"You know, of course, that for the third year running we've topped both the faculty and student rating lists in the AAUB Bulletin. The summer issue has been out for two days now, in case you haven't seen it, and we're miles ahead of anyone else." Sam allowed himself a fleeting smile. "We shouldn't have any complaints about that, but here's the sticker. *Look at Life* must have got an advance copy, because they're after us again to do an on-location article. This time they won't let us off. They're desperate to stay alive and we're hot material."

"Isn't there anything you can do to keep them out of our hair?" Alan asked. They had managed to avoid this twice now, but he had already realized that The Unit would have to submit to the external and internal pressure some day.

"Look, Alan," Sam said patiently, "I've used every excuse and delaying tactic I could scheme up, but there's tremendous pressure now. We've been over the reasons for opening up to public view, and our own reasons for privacy. Now add the fact that at least two people upstairs are suddenly running scared, and willing to cut our throats to get the magafax in here. We have to give in this time."

Alan slouched silently for a moment, then shrugged. The producer was a fiercely competitive man, but his administrative skill, coupled with intense loyalty to his subordinates, ensured that he would know and accept the time when to resist would hurt them more than to submit. The pressure from the public had been steadily growing. They had only been adjusting to the tremendous impact of EVR and home video education, with its attendant costs and staggering change in living patterns, when the next great revolution in education, TriVid, had revitalized, reshaped, and linked the universities and colleges into three great grids. Everybody knew its power, everybody felt the bite, everybody heard students and faculty rave over it, and damned few taxpayers had ever experienced TriVid. The public had a right to be curious; even uneasy and resentful. Alan knew, too, that since the two tottering giants had merged into one magafax, the political power of *Look at Life* had become awesome. If Sam was giving in, then they must really have turned the screws.

"All right," he said. "But I want absolutely silent observation during production. Even in the booth, no questions until after everyone leaves the set." He spoke from hard experience. For some reason they hadn't been able to determine, even during the early days, a visitor anywhere near the set reduced their efficiency. Sam knew it, though he had no real sense of the "dampening" effect The Unit had felt.

"Alan," Sam promised, "I'll do everything I can to make it as remote as possible. When would I ever willingly tamper with an artist's psyche?" And he grinned like a slightly overweight Satan. "Seriously," he continued, "I'll guarantee you two weeks more, but you'd all better start adjusting to the situation, because that's the limit. Sorry to have interrupted you during prime time, but I have a meeting in Toronto this afternoon.' The U. of T. may finally allow the rest of the central-continent grid to join its private network." On that half-humorous note he waved a large hand, and Alan left as the older man dipped into the pile of papers on his desk.

There were papers on Alan's desk too, but he ignored them as he eased his chair to half-recline and closed his eyes. He could visualize his notes readily, and he reviewed them briefly, anticipating the elaboration from point form as he worked the vast student-teacher audience into discussion. When the musical tone sounded he was still mulling over details, and it was with a faint uneasiness that he left his office and strode down to the studio bays.

On set, Alan found the usual state of seeming confusion which, to the experienced eye, meant that everything was working up to the proper fusion for broadcast time. Without cue, and apparently without breaking off their separate activities, The Unit gathered about him for their customary briefing. There were no walk-ons or supers today, but around and above them moved the many technical staff involved with last-minute details. Quickly, incisively, Alan sketched out his new thoughts, while the rest listened attentively, questioning this, adding an idea to that, incorporating everything into the three or four general patterns of interpretation they would follow.

Hunched over in a canvas chair, Ben Bowman scowled ferociously and tested the new inflection in Richard's opening soliloquy. "It's deep, dark, and bloody," he mused, "and certainly suggests the Old Vice or Machiavellian. I like it." He rose and shrugged his hump into place, then limped over to Sylvia Waltham, who stood gracefully listening, toying absently with a solitaire. "Sweet saint, for charity, be not so curst," he leered, then shambled off for some touches to his makeup.

Sylvia smiled, slipped off her ring, and dropped it into Alan's pocket as she gave him a swift kiss on the cheek and whispered,

"Dinner tonight, not overtime." Alan watched her fondly as she glided off into the semi-gloom, admiring for a split second the sheer beauty of his fiancée. Immediately, however, he was drawn back to business, as Nick Ruzzuto drew him to one side with an air of deep concern.

"I didn't want to mention it while the rest were being briefed," Nick said, "but someone's been tampering with the equipment."

Alan was jolted by the coordinator's words. "You're sure?" he asked, even as he realized with a sinking sensation that the question was unnecessary. Nick was a rarity, a brilliant technician who also understood both dramatic literature and stagecraft. He was not only The Unit's camera coordinator but doubled as a director while Alan was in the booth. Quietly, but surely, he sketched out what had happened.

"Merle called me early this morning," he said, "to tell me about a dream she had last night. She had been arguing with herself over whether it was better to toss it off or to tell someone, but she couldn't forget it. She woke Ben and the two of them lay there and discussed it. As Ben says, you know how uncannily prophetic Merle's dreams can be, so he made her call me. It seems she was in one of those sequences where she could see herself acting. But this time she looked fuzzy—couldn't get focussed—and she kept trying to adjust something, as if she were watching on video, while she got absolutely desperate. Well, she apologized for getting me up early, and I went back to bed. Still, knowing Merle, I figured it wouldn't hurt to come in a little ahead of time and see what I could find." He stopped, and Alan nodded approval.

"I couldn't locate any trouble on a visual check," Nick continued, "but I felt uneasy all the same. So I sat for a while looking at the set. I'd turned up the new lighting and it seemed perfect. As a sort of extra, I decided to monitor it for viewing. I flipped up the cameras, and there it was." He paused, and Alan stirred impatiently. "Bank number two of tricons was off sync. Fuzzy as hell. And I couldn't get a proper adjustment. I had to reset all three cameras, and they had been deliberately tampered with."

Alan turned and surveyed the great bay slowly, carefully. "Do you have any idea at all who it was?" he asked.

Nick looked up into the flies reflectively, strong fingers of one hand kneading the other closed fist. "Whoever it was," he answered, "knew exactly what he was doing. It's a factory setting that was changed—

one that only a first-class technician would think of, or understand. We've only two on our crew, and I'll vouch for both of them."

"Sabotage!" Alan breathed reluctantly. "It has to be someone from outside. But why?"

Nick thrust his hands into his pockets and leaned against a light standard. "Could be lots of reasons," he grunted. "I imagine you can think of more than I can. Meanwhile, we've got work to do. We'd better knock heads about it after the session. How about your office?" Alan nodded and set out pensively for the booth, trying to set this new, disturbing complication to one side so that he could concentrate on the broadcast, now only minutes away.

As the door to the booth swung noiselessly shut, Alan made a final effort to get back on track, to think only of his lecture. He noted that the grips had installed his shelves without disturbing the order of his books. Unlike many of his colleagues, he occasionally used this carefully-selected library during lectures, though they also provided the appearance of a study on the three sides presented to the cameras. Most often, however, he used the scanner mounted under the left side of his desk, connected to the vast computerized microfilm library elsewhere in the complex.

As he seated himself in the simulated "armchair" the bank of lights atilt in his desktop suddenly blinked on—two hundred tiny green lights and thermal switches, each representing a three-hundred-student classroom somewhere in the central third of the North American continent. Below them was a smaller panel of switches by which he could provide any number of viewing combinations.

His eyes swept the six monitor cubicles just above eye level, showing his own image, the set, a special-effects model of Shakespeare's Globe theatre, and two random-choice classrooms which appeared as two appropriate lights turned red. The master monitor also held his image, and he straightened his tunic to watch the images respond. He picked up the miniscule, transparent throat mike and earphone, to hear the chief technician checking out all personnel. A few words to test the sound hookup, some subvocal comments to The Unit, and he was ready. The Globe appeared on the master monitor, doors opening, while a voice introduction overrode Elizabethan fanfare, and then he was on camera.

Immediately oblivious to everything else, Alan deftly picked up the threads of discussion from the previous, first lecture of the semester, integrated leftover questions, and began working into the remaining lecture on *Richard III*. They had covered theme and structure already, and now he was leading quite naturally through the ironic reversals in every element of the play, into the character of Richard himself. As he outlined the similarities of Richard and the Marlovian hero, one of the green lights began to blink, and with casual gesture Alan touched it while he talked. It turned red, and on monitor five an earnest, clean-shaven student appeared, leaning forward in his chair. Alan switched him to broadcast and he asked a pertinent question about Richard's many-sided personality. Switching again, Alan split the image and joined his student. In the viewing cubicles of the classrooms, full-sized and in three dimensions, they would seem real enough to touch, sitting almost facing one another to discuss the problem.

It was clear that this student favoured the psychological approach to the character, and when Alan caught several other lights blinking he was relieved to bring another student into confrontation with the young man. By good fortune, this one was full of information on the cycle-play Vice figure, and Alan was pleased to let them hammer out their theories for a few minutes. Choosing the most opportune time, he tactfully suggested that they watch how their ideas worked out in practice, and the two students' images faded to be replaced by that of Ben Bowman, now every inch the complex Duke of Gloucester. Ben went through the opening soliloquy twice, revealing the truth, and the limitations, of each interpretation. No other light blinked, and Alan continued, carrying the discussion into the area of Richard's powers of persuasion. It was easy enough to work interplay now, with the students enthusiastic and participating fully, and they moved, as planned, through argument to illustrative acting to debate between students.

Near the final moments of the programme a question arose involving a scene between Richard and ex-queen Elizabeth in Act IV. The issue was rapidly narrowed to two interpretations. Ben and his wife Merle had gone through both of these when, suddenly, Alan found himself saying, "Isn't there a third possibility here? The Queen has lost husband and both sons. Couldn't she be weakened by grief, like Anne?" He could feel the consternation on set, even as he himself wondered what had possessed him to ask the question. They had never discussed this alternative, and to provide it meant backtracking to the beginning of the scene where Queen Elizabeth, Queen Margaret, and the Duchess of York lament together.

He breathed a sigh of relief as he saw Merle appear, with Olga Brandt as Margaret, and Sylvia with a cloak thrown over her costume to play the Duchess. The Unit worked it through, and admittedly it was not an unreasonable possibility, but it put the final touch to a morning full of unpleasant shocks for Alan. He made an effort to pull himself together and managed to finish off the lecture, concentrating on most of the uncovered material and holding discussion to a minimum. As the monitors went dead he sank back limply and pushed a hand through his hair, surely more grey at the temples, he thought with a grimace. He had been upset by all the intrusions and complications, but was that the real reason for his strange behaviour? The more he considered it, the less certain he was that the idea he had voiced was—could possibly be—his own.

● ●

The view *was* particularly fine this evening, Alan admitted reluctantly. The full, strong moon rode just beyond a school of small, puffball clouds, lighting the gently rolling landscape westward, it seemed, to the very horizon. From the lofty terrace where he and Sylvia sat, the unbroken sweep was breathtaking, almost like an illusion created from an old travel film. Behind them there was only a faint murmur of sound from "Central's" dinner club, yet it was enough to remind Alan of all that had occurred during the day; enough to make him begrudge his admission about the weather to Sylvia. She hadn't yet asked about the morning's broadcast, but he knew she was disturbed and curious. There was just the trace of a line of concern at the corners of her deep violet eyes, and though her chatter was light and humorous, her hand moved too often under her long, jet-black hair to push it back off her shoulder. With a shrug and a half-sigh, he decided it would be as well to straighten out his own thoughts by talking them over.

"You know," he said, groping for his words, "how things sometimes seem to pop up in your mind, and you find yourself saying them as if they'd been there all the time?"

Sylvia nodded, and added, "Yes. It's as if they'd been set out back someplace, getting a part here, a screw tightened there, until, when they're ready, they get thrust out into the middle of everything else." Her lips smiled, but her eyes didn't. "What happened this morning: it wasn't like that, though, was it? And it wasn't like the ideas that we give to one another without talking either. I always hear you say things like that as if they weren't quite—unfamiliar to me." She brushed the knuckles of his hand with a fingertip. "This morning was a shock to me—to all of us."

Alan sat back and relaxed a little, obviously relieved. "I felt quite guilty about it, even while I was talking. I've never pulled anything like that on The Unit." Then he straightened up again. "But you know, I can't explain how it happened, to myself or to you. It felt almost like your finger on my knuckles, or a feather tickling the inside of my head."

"Don't fret too much over it, Alan," Sylvia said earnestly. "Chances are it won't happen again, and if it does—well, we handled it today." She placed her hand over his. "The rest know you too well to think you would trick them or press them without thinking."

Alan answered intensely. "We're all too close for misunderstanding, I know, but the fact is that I did push them. And what's worse, is not having the foggiest notion of how it happened. I can't guarantee that it will never happen again." He leaned forward and said, more quietly yet, "Besides, other things have come piling on, one of them bothersome enough, but to be expected, the other one unexpected and—kind of dirty." And as Sylvia listened silently, a frown growing, he traced over the conversation with Sam about *Look at Life*'s pressure for an article, and Nick's experience with the doctored tricons. "I put off the meeting with Nick," he finished, "because I want Sam to hear it too, tomorrow. Then the three of us can decide on the best action to take." He looked ruefully over their half-eaten meal as a waiter unobtrusively poured wine, then dropped his AP Card on the tray and spun his glass thoughtfully between thumb and forefinger. He was about to speak again when, at a warning glance from Sylvia, he looked up and saw Don Scanlin, another senior lecturer, approaching.

Scanlin, waving a limp hand, dropped loosely into a chair and crossed his long legs restlessly. "Hi, people," he smiled. "Just a week into the semester, and already we're so buried that we hardly meet." He drummed lean fingers on the table. "Why so glum? You haven't been having a lover's spat, have you? Don't call it off or I'll lose my credit in the pool. I've got five on you for an early June wedding."

Sylvia looked somewhat annoyed as she answered, "Really, Don. If there is such a distasteful thing as a pool, I should think people would have better places to put their credits."

Don gave her a broad grin, face wrinkling all the way to his receding hairline. The effect was somewhat startling, since everything seemed to warm except his light grey eyes. "Well," he drawled, "you know what a hothouse atmosphere this is. Can't keep anything to yourself for long. Incidentally," he turned to Alan, "the latest is that something went a little hairy in your studio this morning. I thought that nothing could faze The Unit." There was an almost concealed note of envy in the statement.

Alan felt a sudden touch of ice at the base of his ribs, but there was no outward sign of it as he held his wine to the light and squinted through it. "We had a mild panic," he said. "My fault entirely. I didn't stick to the standard variants. But The Unit came through like the old U.S. Cavalry and saved me from getting scalped."

Sylvia laughed, as Don looked slightly puzzled. "Perhaps it was a good thing, happening so early in the year," she said. "We might have been getting just a little too cocky, too smug. Why, I wouldn't have put it past Alan to engineer something like this just to sharpen us up, though I believe him," she hastily added, "when he says it really was a slip."

Don shifted uneasily in his chair. "Yes," he muttered. "I'm not so sure he didn't plan it, myself." He grinned again, less warmly, as he recrossed his legs. "No such problem in my area," he said briskly. "If you fluff an EVR, you just go back and retape it. I've spent a lot of hours on a single lesson. After all, I can't do less than my best for those thousands of home viewers—one hundred and eighty thousand, I think, this year." There was a hard sound of satisfaction in the last.

Alan did a swift review and said, "That's up over last year, isn't it? And you had a great rating on the Level Two Shakespeare course."

Don flushed slightly. "Yes," he answered. "Somebody out *there* likes me." The emphasis wasn't lost on Sylvia and Alan, who knew well enough that in the profession Level Three work such as theirs had a greater, if unwarranted, prestige. Don rose, and straightened his gaunt frame. "Time to get back," he noted, somewhat sourly. "I've got two graduate students moving in next week, and my wife insists that we're having a party that weekend. Late hours for me."

Alan and Sylvia rose too, as Alan pulled a long face. "That's food for indigestion," he said. "My students aren't due for a while yet, but I've got some thesis drafts sitting on the desk already." Don waved again and ambled off, while the waiter appeared and returned Alan's card. Together, he and Sylvia made their way silently to Alan's quarters across the complex, both pensive and subdued now.

It was Sylvia who broached the matter that was troubling them, when they had settled for a brief nightcap. "Do you think," she asked, "that he was asking about the flurry over your slip?"

Alan shrugged noncommittally. "I couldn't tell," he answered. "The first thought that came to me, though, was the tricon tampering. I just don't know what he was after."

Sylvia moved closer and slid his arm over her shoulder. "Perhaps it's unjust, but I don't really trust him," she said, looking uncomfortable. "No. It would be better to say I don't trust his wife. She's so ambitious for him." She moved Alan's hand down a little. "Are we invited to this party?" she asked.

Alan took a last sip of his drink and said thoughtfully, "I expect we will be. It would be politic to invite us. And it would be doubly politic to go," he added. "And now," he tried to copy Ben's best leer, "since there's a lot to do tomorrow, suppose we just relax for what's left of the evening." There was no more conversation.

Next morning Alan rose even earlier than usual. He carried breakfast to his desk and began an intense review of *Richard II* in preparation for the Saturday morning conference with The Unit. This time he didn't want any unexpected interpretations, and he cross-checked a number of the standard editions of his own ultramicrofiche cards, even dialling the library once or twice for a look at recent articles on microfilm. Before leaving, he phoned and made a late-morning appointment with Nick and Sam, then hastily put his notes together and made for the pedexpress. He was still figuring blocking for some key scenes as he entered BC and dropped to the studio area. It would be a very busy day.

The Unit seemed more amused by the events of the past day than anything else, Alan found to his relief—at least until he told them, in confidence, about the mechanical mischief that Nick had uncovered. Olga had laughingly tossed her thick braids and preened over getting some extra "tube time", but later, Alan noticed, she sought out Nick during a break and, together with Merle, talked very seriously with him. Paul Jacobs, the last of the "secret seven", as they sometimes humorously called themselves, hadn't even been on set the day previous, and he clearly was upset as he listened to a summary by Ben Bowman. Then, as they got deep into the day's work, the whole matter seemed to have been forgotten.

Paul and Ben were working up a fine contrast as Bolingbroke and Richard II, respectively; Paul using a strong, cold, businesslike manner, and Ben a soft, almost effeminate, musical voice and overly graceful gestures. Blocking went smoothly, almost entirely controlled by Nick, showing his superb sense of action focus; dialogue patterns were tested and built in corners; discussions surfaced everywhere now and then—in short, it looked like the usual seeming chaos of a perfect rehearsal. Only The Unit itself would have been aware that there was a fraction of attention elsewhere; that now there was hardly a second when someone of the group wasn't keeping the rest of the set under watch.

How like them, Alan thought, simply to evolve it like that, without prearrangement, and he found suddenly that he had been terrifically tense for the last hour or so. Now he felt that everyone had taken a share of his anxiety and dissipated it.

It was the same in Sam's office, later on, when Nick and Alan filled him in on what had happened. Sam was incredulous in the first instant, and in the next he had accepted the facts and was ready to work out some strategy.

"There are two directions we can move in, it seems to me," he said crisply as he drew a line down a sheet of paper. "Nick, you can check back to see who's been temporary on your crew for the last year, and who might have been permanent even before that. In addition, you can pass the word to those you trust, and tighten up set-checks during and after rehearsal. Bring a few crew on early before broadcast, and use a fine-tooth comb on the equipment. It's a pity we can't give you the set entirely for yourselves, but we have to keep the afternoon and evening courses booked in." He finished jotting his remarks in the first column.

"I'll do some quiet looking and talking upstairs," he continued. "I can check crew for the other two courses as well, and I'll see if I can't get a little extra security without making it too obvious. As for the changes during broadcast, well, you'll have to look after that yourself, Alan."

As the others got up to leave, he stood up and said, "Oh, there's something further you'd better know now. I'm not sure it has anything at all to do with this, but someone is trying very hard to move me off the course, and into liaison with the University of Toronto. It might have been flattering under other circumstances, but now I'd better look at the apple and see if there's a worm in it." He placed a hand on Alan and Nick's shoulders as they left the office. "Meanwhile, think Iago rather than Othello, eh?" He closed the door with a grim chuckle.

The rest of the day was uneventful, and Alan finished work a little earlier than usual. He and Sylvia spent the evening pleasantly enough with the Bowmans, where, by common consent, none of them spoke of the problems facing them. Bidding was brisk, the play was sharp, and they went through seven rubbers of bridge to end with a difference of only fifty points. The change of mental pace seemed like a tonic, and Sunday Alan and Sylvia spent the entire day picnicking off in the forest belt, drinking in the beauty and the brisk fall air as if to store them up for the whole winter.

On Monday, everything went off like clockwork, and by broadcast time on Tuesday they were all beginning to wonder if they'd been too panicky about last Friday's events.

In the booth, Alan felt he was really peaked for his lecture. Checkout had gone smoothly, all equipment was functioning perfectly, he had worked through the introductory material and was discussing the conflicting opinions on the unevenness of *Richard II*. He had provoked strong class reaction to the view that Shakespeare was experimenting with the portrayal of two social orders in the play, and The Unit had demonstrated, admirably, the two kinds of poetry and action. Ben was a beautifully weak Richard, last of a declining line of medieval kings, and Paul was a dynamic Henry, the epitome of the renaissance man.

A student was on now, asking about Henry's apparently inconsistent use of the old-style rhetoric in Act V, scene iii, and Alan, anticipating a close look at the text, thumbed his microfilm scanner. Nothing happened. Throwing a glance to the monitor, he tried again. Same result. The student had now finished his question and was looking expectant, and no lights blinked. Without waiting, Alan put himself on, and with a casual motion reached across to one of his shelves, plucking down a copy of *Richard II*.

Playing it for effect, he opened to the scene and smoothed down the page with a caressing hand. It was partly from a genuine love, and partly because he knew the regard these students had for real books. Instead of calling on Paul, he read himself, throwing into it the exaggerated style which a sarcastic Henry would use in dealing with his elderly aunt and uncle. He could see, through the narrow glass across the front of his booth, the reaction of The Unit, Merle kissing her hand to him and curtsying, Paul with a head-back laugh and fists on his hips. It went ideally, and the moment was past. "Out of the woods again," he thought, as he switched to another student, and they were

off on a new track. The imagery of grief came now, and without forcing.

It was a fine class this year, if the first few lectures were any indication. They reached out after material on the barest hint. He answered,
piecing together a number of lines, and using The Unit for a few more
spot illustrations. That ought to do it. And then, with a shock that
pinned him to his chair, he heard what was surely his own voice,
asking—"Yet, can we take all this talk of grief imagery seriously when
the Queen speaks of it as she does in Act II, scene ii? The beginning
seems all right, but what about the end?"

It couldn't have been worse, was his first thought. Every producer
cuts those lines, simply because no actress wants to tangle with them.
On the set, six faces stared up at him in stunned amazement. Then
Sylvia moved quickly to Nick and picked up the master text. Sitting
in the massive throne, she opened the huge book, found the page, and
nodded. Alan switched her in as she appeared in monitor 2, a pathetic,
almost ridiculous figure, dwarfed by book and throne. Ben gave the
cue, off-camera: " ' 'Tis nothing but conceit, my gracious lady,' " and
Sylvia read in a small, slightly pitiful voice:

> 'Tis nothing less: conceit is still derived
> From some forefather grief; mine is not so,
> For nothing hath begot my something grief;
> Or something hath the nothing that I grieve;
> 'Tis in reversion that I do possess;
> But what it is, that is not yet known; what
> I cannot name; 'tis nameless woe, I wot.

It was more than adequate—it was very good. Nevertheless, it was
absolutely clear that while the grief imagery in the play wouldn't be
harmed by the lines, they were a poetic blunder on Shakespeare's
part. The students were facing their first real proof that the young
Shakespeare could write a few bad lines.

Picking up that idea, Alan finished the last few minutes of the
lecture by extemporizing, even reading one or two other tortured con-
ceits and "flat" lines. When the monitors went dead, he wiped cold
sweat from his forehead and walked shakily down on to the set. He
stood looking at The Unit, who all had a pinched, frightened appearance.

It was Merle who spoke first. "Alan, I'd say twice was too much,
but—that wasn't you, I mean, that was you, and it wasn't. Oh, I don't
know quite what I mean."

Paul followed her. "I heard you just as clearly as anyone else, Alan. A little mechanical, maybe, as if you had a sore jaw. But what bothers me is that I had just moved off to arrange my ruff. I didn't have my earphone in, Alan."

● ● ●

The rest of the studio was dark now, save for a pool of light just inside the double doors, under which one of Nick's technicians had moved a tricon dolly to "make some adjustments". No one would enter unobserved. The Unit came together at the back of the set. It had been a minor anticlimax when Nick and Alan examined the scanner in the booth, to find that the power supply module had been pulled just far enough to break contact. Their real problem was to explain the strange voice which had once again threatened to disrupt their broadcoast. They were all agreed now that Alan hadn't actually spoken the words that they, and the network apparently, had heard. "I'm fairly certain," Alan was saying, "that the first time I did speak. This time, no! I didn't even sub-voc, yet it went to you all. For me that rules out any kind of electronic feed-in. What do you say, Nick?"

Nick threw up his hands. "I've heard of projectors that could do the job in a limited space like the studio—even into the booth. But it went network too. That would mean too complicated a setup to be concealed. It's nothing that I could explain in terms of existing equipment, under these circumstances."

There was a painful silence, until Paul cleared his throat self-consciously. "Look," he said, "I'm the one who heard it without my phone, and I've been trying to remember exactly what the sensation was. You can call the mindpatchers if you want, but I'm convinced that I didn't even hear it in the usual sense. It was inside, like moth-wings against my brain."

There was a stir through the group, and he burst out defensively: "Come on. Some of us have volunteered for the psi-fi boys, and we know they've uncovered some pretty weird things. You, Nick! You can box the compass spinning on your head at the bottom of a well. Merle! How many of your dreams turn out to be wrong? Alan! Why haven't you let them run tests on you? You radiate like an emotion furnace. We can all tell when you're happy, excited, angry, or concentrating, from as far away as your office." He folded his arms and scowled. "If it isn't psi, then we're all crazy."

Olga dropped Nick's hand and stood up. "No one's disagreeing, Paul," she said quietly, "At least I'm not. Maybe we just don't want to accept it unless there's no other explanation."

The others murmured assent, and Ben spoke up. "As long as I wasn't the first to bring it up, I'll climb on your wagon. That voice was a near-perfect imitation, but it wasn't Alan. Yet it was more a lack of proper inflection than wrong voice quality. I don't know of an impersonator alive who would duplicate a voice that way. The closest I've heard was a tape of faked confessions in the East-West Non-War Archives. They had spliced thousands of single words to make statements."

He shifted uneasily and Sylvia continued. "Nick has already ruled out anything like that. I agree that it wasn't Alan speaking, or even thinking, for that matter. He doesn't put thoughts together like that." She smiled encouragement at Paul. "So that leaves Paul's theory. And now, what do we do about it?"

Alan waited for a moment, until it was clear that no one was about to add anything or make a suggestion. "From my own experience with this 'voice' or whatever we call it, I'd be inclined to agree that it couldn't have been gadgetry. You know that I don't discount psi, but I haven't gone overboard for it either. Still, since I can't find any reasonable theory other than Paul's—let's assume that it is some kind of telepathy." He looked up as Sam slipped in at the far end of the studio, waited until he had moved up on to the set, and continued. "Number one. If it's a telepath, then I'll guarantee that no matter how the interference works it's a student somewhere in the network. The questions or suggestions are thoughtful and sincere; exactly what you would expect from a student who's really interested but hasn't got a broad background. Number two. It almost certainly couldn't be anyone in Television Central. For one thing, if it were tied up with the sabotage that's going on, it would have had a technical basis. For another, if it were anyone on the academic end, he would know too much for that kind of question to occur to him." Sam looked rather quizzical, but he seemed to have caught the significance of Alan's comments.

"All right, then," Alan stated flatly, "we have a telepathic student, out there anywhere in a five- or six-hundred-mile radius. One of sixty thousand. How do we locate that student? And what do we work out to prevent chaos while we're looking?" He watched while The Unit mulled it over, talking quietly. Sam leaned impassively against a flat, obviously biding his time until all the pieces fell into place.

Finally Ben straightened up from alongside Merle and said: "Paul mentioned the psi people and *their* tests. Doesn't the Basic Graduate Entrance Battery have a set of psychological exams in it?" He glanced at Sam. "Why couldn't we get the Big Brain to run a search on the students enrolled in our course? A check for latent psi possibilities?"

Sam stroked his chin thoughtfully. "You've been away from teaching for a long time, Ben," he answered. "I'll give it a try, but I don't think the exams are designed to reveal that sort of thing. There's another possibility though." He thrust his hands into his tunic pockets. "If there's anything like that in records, it would be in the Continental Computer banks. Lord knows how deep it goes when it takes the initial personality pattern at birth. There hasn't been a pirate scanner built yet that can read the whole imprint off an AP Card." He turned to Alan as he wiped sweat off his palms. "Let me look into both areas and see what can be done. Telepath, yet," he muttered. "Next you'll be creating a Phantom of BC. I gather that your mysterious marvel has struck again." He held up a hand as Alan turned. "Don't tell me now," he said. "Let me get started on my hunt for the proverbial needle. Come up to the office when you've figured out how to keep your lectures to yourselves." With that, he strode off.

The set seemed abnormally quiet after Sam had left. Then Sylvia spoke up. "Alan," she asked, "is it possible for you to override this voice somehow? I mean, suppose you tried to speak yourself while it was speaking?"

Alan shook his head. "No," he answered, "I don't know whether I could or not, and it would certainly make for confusion all around. Who could tell which was me—and what would I say? It would be better to have nothing at all." He snapped his fingers and swung around. "Maybe that's it. Nick, is it possible for us to cut the audio when that voice comes on? It seems to operate through me, somehow, and feed into the network. Or better still, could you cut out the booth just for that length of time? Wire in a switch for me? Wipe off the video too. Complete isolation at a touch."

Nick nodded assent. "It would take only a few patches," he said. "I think you'd better have control yourself, too. Of course, we'll catch hell for it, you know, if we blank the channel for more than a half-second. But I guess that would be better than complete ruin."

The rest of The Unit looked relieved, and Alan checked them with a gesture. "Remember," he warned them, "that this is only a temporary measure. The next time that voice butts in, I want every one of you concentrating on it. Anything we can find out about it, or any way we can use to stop it, that's what we all need to look for." Somewhat chastened, they broke up the meeting and wandered off in their separate ways.

The next two days went normally, save for the extra tension which was almost tangible on set during rehearsals. Alan's switch was installed immediately, and tested. Nick cued in an automatic tape run of The Globe to cover with, and they decided it would serve if it was necessary. Meanwhile, Sam had gone digging, and had a fair amount of information when he, Alan, and Nick met in his office late Thursday afternoon.

"First," he opened, "the matter of student records. As I thought, there isn't anything in the Entrance Exams which would help us at all. They were designed to discover study patterns and potential problems in students who might need special help. Counselling says anything else uncovered is inviolable, and concerns abnormalities in social adjustment. A psi may well be maladjusted, but it would still require too much personal contact to check such cases out." He picked up another official memo. "Second, the continental computer people say we'd need a writ from the International Court to get anything other than credit or task proficiency ratings. Even the Americanadian Government has limited access." He leaned back and put his hands behind his head. "Third, I've picked up a few scraps that point towards one individual behind the technical sabotage. Nothing definite to go on, just who's been pally with who lately, and hints of dissatisfaction with present assignments. I may find out a bit more on Saturday night, when I'm forced to socialize for a change." His lips pursed distastefully on the last. Sam didn't like big parties.

Alan smiled as a sudden thought struck him. "You've been invited to the Scanlin's party too."

Sam's eyes narrowed as he said, "Yes. Call it overtime. If you're going, be discreet but keep looking and listening." Alan felt a prickling at the back of his neck remembering what he and Sylvia had said. As he met Sam's eyes, he knew who Sam was talking about.

Nick cleared his throat. "Have fun, you people. I'm just hired help, so I don't rate an invitation." He grinned. "Guess I'll just have to struggle through a quiet evening with an old friend."

Alan grinned back. "Tell Olga that there's a fine concert on at Regional Arts."

"Seriously," Nick said, "I've checked out the technical staff, and there are only two possibilities among them. One has only been with us for this semester, and the other has been gone from our set for six months. The first one should have had his first class papers long ago, but keeps moving from place to place. Doesn't get along with his chiefs. The second one made first class this summer, and definitely wants to move up to coordinator. He's someplace in EVR now, getting sequence experience."

Alan glanced at Sam, who said quietly, "Let me have his name, and I'll look into it. You keep an eye on your new man." He rummaged about on his desk, picked up a correspondence cartridge, and clipped it into the viewer. "Latest on the *Look at Life* visit," he grunted. "We have a definite time now. The team will be here from Wednesday to Friday, two weeks from now. They'll follow the complete workup of one lecture. Rafferty is the interviewer. Very tough, very shrewd, very meticulous. But also very impartial. It's a good break, I think. Most say they forgot he was there until the direct conversations. Anyway, it's the best I could do." On that note, Alan and Nick left, each wondering what tomorrow's broadcast would bring.

It was too good to be true. They were not far from the end of the lecture now, and it had been a beautiful broadcast. Perhaps because they were all so keyed up, the atmosphere had been literally charged. The Unit had outdone themselves on the interpretations—Paul, for example, had been fantastic in Richard's death scene. There was no room for debate after he had shown the histrionic poet-philosopher bemoaning his fate, galvanized into action too late, revealing a tremendously tragic glimpse of latent, fiery majesty. There was a brief pause while the recognition of wasted potential was absorbed, then a deluge of student response. Alan would have congratulated himself, but he knew too well that the first two disturbances had come near the end of broadcast time. He was, however, almost two people right now; the first intensely involved with the discussion, providing answers, pulling students together, and the second coolly detached, watching, waiting.

When it finally happened he reacted so swiftly that the total elapsed time was a mere four seconds. Then they were back on and he was smoothly finishing the summary. Two minutes later they were off the network and he was out of the booth and bounding down on to the set. Most of the technical people were unaware that anything serious had happened, and Alan was sure that the break had simply appeared to be a transmission problem through the network. The

Unit came babbling together, full of information and comment, not exactly jubilant, but excited because at last they had something to go on. As they quieted down, Alan swiftly began to assemble what they had learned.

"To begin with," he said, "we know for sure that it wasn't me."

Sylvia interrupted with—"Maybe four words, Alan. Four or five sounded like you."

"I hit the switch," he answered, "by the second word, I'm sure." The voice had begun asking a question, something like "Isn't there a textual problem here, on page . . . "

Paul jumped in with: "It was 'on page' where the change came. And then a mumbled apology. I heard it distinctly."

Olga was literally bouncing in her eagerness to speak. "A girl! It's a girl. You could hear the voice changing when she realized she'd made a mistake. Whatever it was she thought she saw, when she got confused, embarrassed I think, her own voice came through."

Alan held up both hands to calm them. "That's what I was going to point out. When I cut the booth out, it did cut the voice off the network, but the change itself only came when she got flustered. Now, the big question that occurs to me is—does she know what she's been doing?"

There were shiftings and murmurings, but no one spoke up. Then Nick said, "I'm not sure about that. Wouldn't it be hard for her not to know? I mean, to make you ask the question she wants to ask— wouldn't that be too much of a coincidence if the thing were subconscious?"

Sylvia shrugged eloquently. "When Alan says something I've been thinking, I don't find it unusual. I suppose if you found people around you doing it all the time, you might get an inferiority complex, but you might also think that's just the way the world is."

Alan said shrewdly, "It's a question for a phychiatrist, at least, if not a psi researcher. But Nick, that wasn't all you were going to tell us."

Nick looked somewhat uncomfortable. "I suppose," he grumbled, "as long as we're taking this telepathy seriously, I might as well go all the way." He laced his fingers together and bent them back till the knuckles cracked. "You see, I can stand here and point in her direction." He stretched out an arm, roughly northwest Alan guessed, and stood rigid.

Nobody laughed. No one even smiled. Instead, Merle said to him,

"I can go you one better. She's near-sighted. Real thick glasses." As she spoke, Alan called up a hazy, quick vision from the back of his mind, from the instant when his hand remained on the switch and he realized that the voice had faded, was finished. The image had been blurred, almost unreadable, until it drew into focus as if someone had adjusted a projector lens: it was a page of the assigned play, *Richard II.* At that point the voice had faltered, changed, and apologized. Merle continued. "She's young, nearsighted, and scared silly of the people around her. I only hope we haven't lost her."

Sylvia sighed softly. "I was nearly staggered by a terrible feeling of frightened loneliness." She put her hand on Alan's arm. "I don't know if you felt it too, but I'm absolutely certain that she doesn't mean to cause us any trouble. And please, no matter how difficult it makes things for us, let's try not to hurt her." The rest all agreed, obviously, naturally, and Alan himself felt that they would have to be extremely careful in handling the situation. But come what may, they would have to find her, and soon too, very soon.

● ● ● ●

They had finished a sober and very quiet dinner in Alan's apartment and were watching a massive line of thunderheads move relentlessly towards them across the plains. Sylvia had snuggled close, as if for protection from the elements, though both of them knew it was actually because of the threatening situation that neither could put aside. Then she sat up and pushed at her hair with a self-conscious laugh. "I was going to say that the weather reminded me of Act Three of *Lear,*" she said, "and then I suddenly realized how much this thing has grown on us. When you put our problems alongside the play, though, they take on a little different perspective, don't they?"

Alan, who had been making exactly the same comparison, answered, "Yes. And not only do they look a lot smaller, but I was thinking of how much better off Lear would have been with Sam and The Unit to help him."

Sylvia laughed whole-heartedly at that. "Can you picture Sam as Lear's Fool?"

Alan couldn't help smiling too at the vision of Sam in motley, but then he became serious again. "It's incredible that so much has happened in so short a time. But the main point that occurred to me was that we've never let this paralyze us. So far we've managed to cope, and even anticipate a little, even if we haven't solved anything."

Sylvia rose and began absently to leaf through the tape listings, then dialled a Segovia as Alan tossed over his AP Card. "I'd be a lot happier," she said, "if we could get just one problem out of the way. Find out who's behind the sabotage, or be certain that Sam won't have to leave us. Get the *Look at Life* crew here and gone. Any of them is enough to worry about, without our uninvited guest wreaking havoc during broadcasts." She picked off a cassette as it came through the slot, and slipped it into the console.

Alan paced restlessly in front of the window, not yet soothed by the quiet guitar sounds that floated through the room. "We may not have disposed of any yet," he said more optimistically, "but Sam or Nick will have something new by tomorrow." As if it were a cue line, the door tone sounded, and Alan opened to find a smiling Nick *and* Sam waiting.

"Come look at my preety peecture," Nick smirked, as he twirled an imaginary moustache. He moved to the low table in front of the couch and unfolded a large map of the mid-continental grid. As the others gathered round he placed his scriber on Television Central.

"Now, considering that I took this down and laid it out on the studio floor first to get the direction, we have a very interesting development." He traced a light line northwest, into the prairie province area of Old Canada. "Depending on how accurately my location sense works, we have from three to eight possible classrooms. I personally feel that I could pinpoint the direction to within three degrees, but say five to be sure. That way we have Beatrice, Bassett, Pierre, Rapid City, Miles City, Willeston, Bismark, and perhaps Minot or Regina. I'd almost swear, though, that it's Beatrice, Bassett, or Miles City."

Alan stared intently at the map, mind racing furiously ahead. "How do we narrow them down for certain?" he asked, more to himself than anybody. "Do we have to visit each one personally during class time? And could we spot our girl that way?"

Sam had been watching with an amused expression, and now he slapped Alan on the back and said heartily, "We might not have to do half as much looking as you think. We were so busy trying the far-out places, like our Big Brain and the Continental Computer, that we missed the most obvious. You talked on set about the psi-fi tests that some of you have taken right here. Well, as it happens, they're running a battery through the whole network. They've done students and faculty in the whole of the southwestern and northwestern quadrants, grid unit by unit, and are working on the northeastern now."

Sylvia had been listening with growing excitement, but now she frowned. "I suppose that their records are closed too, and we're right back where we started from."

"Already checked that," Sam grinned. "They won't give out names, but they will tell us if there are any high-potential psi cases in each of the eight classrooms that we've pinpointed. Even give some indication of which are latent telepaths. The well-developed cases are long since down here on special scholarships."

"How soon can they give us the information?" Alan asked.

"Monday morning," Sam replied briskly. "And by then, I expect we should have worked up a method of identifying the student absolutely." He moved to the door as Nick followed, folding his map. "See you at Scanlin's party," he said somewhat regretfully, and he and Nick were gone.

"Identifying her is one thing, Alan," Sylvia mused as they went slowly back to the couch, "but how we'll contact her and what will happen after that are the things that really bother me."

Alan reached out and set the lighting to "Fade off", then gave her knee a pat. "I'll work on that over the weekend myself," he reassured her. "It seems to be my job personally, since she works through me. And I'll try to be as warm and friendly as possible."

"Not too warm, now," Sylvia said archly, putting his hand back on her knee. "I'll bet she has a crush on you already." Beyond the window, the storm broke in magnificent fury, but now it was not really threatening. It was stimulating, exhilarating, as it crashed through the strains of guitar music still pulsing in the background.

The music pulsing in the background next evening was of a far different sort, and it added a great deal to the confusion and noise of the Scanlin's party. It was like something out of the 1970s, with a trio of live "musicians" in one corner and a real, professional bartender in another. He was hand-mixing drinks from a disconnected autobar, and Alan had to admit that his own tasted better than the standard dial mix. The Scanlins had rented the social room in their court, and were really laying it on. "Now I believe those rumours about her family's perpetual credit reserves," Sylvia remarked candidly, as she gazed across the crowded room to where Deborah Scanlin stood poised in a circle of admiring males, talking with languid gestures that shifted the planes of her see-around dress.

"No law of compensation working there," Alan muttered over his glass. "She's loaded with credits, and everything else too." Even from this distance one could see that the body behind the dress was as beautiful as the face above it. As they watched, Mrs. Scanlin caught sight of them over a male shoulder, said something which drew a burst of laughter, blew a kiss to her admirers and worked her way gracefully through the tangle of guests to them.

"Good evening, people," she tinkled at them. "Having a good time? My, it doesn't seem that long, but I'll bet we haven't met face to face for over a year. But I have the advantage there. I see you two or three times a week."

Alan looked surprised. "You mean to say you watch the lectures?" he asked.

"Wouldn't miss them," she replied. "I find the viewing rooms a great way to pass the time between vacations. And they are a bit more educational than Com Vid, aren't they? Yours is especially fascinating, of course. After all, we all—you, Don, me—we all love Shakespeare." If one were listening closely, the superficial playgirl banter slipped a fraction at the close.

Sylvia's manner was open, almost ingenuous. "Why, it's lovely to meet someone who really watches because she wants to, and not because she has to." Deborah's eyes narrowed, and Alan waited with concealed amusement for the sparring to end and the battle to begin. It was clear that these two weren't fooling one another. There was strong hostility deep beneath the amiable chitchat. And Alan felt too that Deborah's manner was a bit like her dress. You got a thousand fragmentary glimpses of the naked mind behind it, yet not enough to prove what was abundantly clear. It might have been an interesting few minutes, but Don Scanlin suddenly appeared, uneasy and overly-pleasant, to welcome them and point out mutual friends. Newcomers interrupted, and Alan and Sylvia took the opportunity to move away and mingle with the other guests.

Time passed quickly enough, and they found, rather surprisingly, that even in the close association of the Complex they were meeting people they hadn't spoken to for ages. Gradually, however, Alan realized that the administrators, of whom there were few, came mainly from the TriVid sector, and he wondered if anyone else saw the possible significance of it. He noted, as well, that Deborah paid special attention to these people. He had about decided that they would learn nothing else of importance, and had come to the bar for one last set of drinks, when he found himself pinned behind two of these officials, deeply engrossed in their own conversation. He listened unabashedly while he waited his turn, as one of them said spiritedly, "I want to look at it soon. It's a whole new prospectus for the Shakespeare course, and Scanlin has some good ideas."

The other laughed jovially and said, "Oh, come off it. A minute ago you were telling me you're getting bored here and might take an offer from World Communications. Just between us, Josh, is it a coincidence that Deborah Scanlin's family has a big chunk of credit reserves from that corporation?" Alan got his drinks and didn't wait to be seen by them. Perhaps he couldn't avoid it, but eavesdropping was still eavesdropping. Yet it was a very juicy piece of information to chew over, and later, when they had left the party, he and Sylvia decided that the pieces made a fairly obvious pattern. It was pretty clear that the Scanlins were mounting a strong campaign to get Don into TriVid, and that the Shakespeare course was their objective.

"I can't prove it, Alan," Sylvia said, "but I have the distinct feeling that it's mainly Deborah's idea. Don no doubt wants it, but don't you think he's being pushed?"

Alan paused thoughtfully as they reached Sylvia's apartment door. "His actions would surely give that impression. If he were the mastermind, or even an equal conspirator, you'd think he would be at least as confident and devious as Deborah in public. After all, there's a good bit of ham actor in all of us lecturers, and you've got to concede that he's a first-rate one."

As they stood in the open doorway, Sylvia shivered and took his arm. "Stay?" she asked a trifle plaintively, and he nodded silently.

Monday proved to be a hectic day, as The Unit prepared the first broadcast on *Henry IV, Part I.* They had actually spent a good part of Sunday in Alan's apartment, mapping out much of what they would normally have discussed on set, and Alan had found himself fighting a tendency on everybody's part to change his usual approaches in order to cover any conceivable question. Finally he had called a halt. "We will not be stampeded," he said severely, "into changing the format that we've developed over such a long time, and with such hard work. If the girl does interrupt, we'll cover as best we can, but we owe it to the other students to stick to the methods they've begun to learn and use themselves." There was an uncomfortable pause, and then general if somewhat shamefaced agreement.

After that they had settled down to the usual intense, thoroughly integrated routine that characterized The Unit. But if they had thought the extra work would make the next day go more easily, they were mistaken. For one thing, they had to work while additions were being made to the circuitry. Alan's booth became a beehive of activity by nine o'clock, when the psi-fi report revealed that only two of the eight classrooms had female latent telepaths. Taking the chance that no others had been overlooked, Nick and Alan decided to set two of the monitors on open circuit to the Bassett and Miles City classrooms. Alan would be able to keep them both under observation during the broadcast, and even control the tricons for scan and close-up right from the booth, overriding the classroom cameramen.

"We'll get you a little practice late tonight," Nick said, "and I can leave it patched for the broadcast in the morning. Now we'd better clear the mess away for the afternoon people." Ben had been doubling for both Nick and Alan at times through the morning, and the strain showed in all their faces as they left.

Instead of a leisurely lunch, however, Alan found himself summoned to Sam's office. "Sit down and hear some mixed news," Sam told him. "Do you want the good or the bad first?"

Alan slumped down and stretched his legs. "Give me the good first," he sighed. "I don't think I could take the bad just yet."

Sam chose a cigar from his private stock, lit up and puffed away with relish, and leaned forward. "You probably didn't miss me at the party," he said with false modesty, "but I was back in Toronto. The government advanced our trial budget date by two weeks last Friday night, and there was an emergency meeting Saturday. U. of Toronto has been playing coy with us and the Eastern grid, and suddenly it was time to decide. Well, after the usual few hours of horsing around, I threw in a little surprise. I gave them a half-hour argument on why U. of T. belonged in the East Coast grid. For a minute it almost backfired, because they both decided to have a look in the gift horse's mouth. But it worked." He grinned triumphantly. "After all," he added, "why shouldn't it have worked? It was the only proper and workable solution in the first place."

Alan smiled his approval. "And so Sam Meynard, middle-aged prodigy, remains as the wonder producer of Television Central. Tremendous!" The glow of admiration didn't have much chance to settle over Alan, however, as he remembered the way Sam had greeted him. "All right," he said. "We've finally got one problem out of our hair. Now what's the bad news?" Sam grudgingly dropped his air of victory and slid a memo over the desk to Alan. Alan read silently, looked speculatively at the memo for a moment, and then passed it back with a soft whistle. "This one could be real trouble, or it could be straightened out in a few minutes. It depends on who's pushing, the union or someone upstairs." The matter was quite clear and simple. The union had complained that Nick was performing duties not covered in terms of contract. He could either be a director or a camera coordinator, but not both. If his status was not established at once, they would pull all cameramen off set. Less clear was an implied threat of action because of the previous breaches of contract, and it was to this that Alan referred, as Sam understood.

"It's technically my decision," he said, "but I leave it entirely up to you. Is he ready?"

Alan rose wearily to his feet. "He's been ready for a year," he replied. "But it was ideal to have him coordinating as well. I only hope his replacement is half as good."

Sam reached for the phone. "I'll get his new contract sent down. You tell Nick about his promotion, and check his opinion of that first-bank cameraman. If Nick likes him and the union OK's it, we'll move him up temporarily until he writes his first-class papers—this weekend. Meanwhile, I'll softsoap some of my friends on the union executive. If no one has been bought off we may get out of it easily."

As Sam placed his first call, Alan drifted out, wondering whether to skip lunch, get at the pile of work in his office, go back to his quarters and read thesis drafts, or write a fable about changing new problems for old. The strain was beginning to tell.

Tuesday morning the air fairly crackled with anticipation. Alan began by introducing the Elizabethan cyclical view of history, along with the theory that Shakespeare had wanted to write a complete cycle of the Wars of the Roses from his first play. He used The Unit to test the notion that one play anticipated another, and they skipped back and forth from play to play. The students were well-prepared and sceptical, and the discussion moved off the subject for the present, into the "facts" of history that the bard had found in the chronicles and skillfully trimmed or expanded for good drama. This led to the last progression, the function of characters, and Alan masterfully directed and restrained the discussion so that they reached climax just short of examining the incomparable Falstaff. Then the broadcast was over, as planned. There had been no interruption!

They reacted first with almost hysterical relief, and then slipped rapidly into a mood of depression. The women expressed it first, when Merle wondered aloud whether the girl had been frightened into dropping the course. Alan noted that both classrooms on the monitors had appeared completely filled, but agreed that this didn't prove anything.

Olga said with mixed feelings, "Perhaps she's decided to give up asking questions."

But Sylvia put the situation back into perspective when she replied, "Oh, maybe we're just over-reacting because we women will have to take a back seat for the next broadcast."

That was another sobering thought for Alan, who hadn't really considered the problem of bringing extra men on set for Friday. This play, more than any other of Shakespeare's, was a man's play, and they would be working with people normally outside The Unit. He doubted there would be any difficulty with Jack Kirby, whose superlative Falstaff always worked beautifully opposite Paul's Prince Hal, but he was less secure about their new Hotspur, and the extras of Falstaff's gang. With a sort of mental crossing of fingers he reassured the women that they could all be off-camera, if they wished, and that he would actually prefer that they be there. "After all," he said, "we don't want to break the magic circle." The others left with somewhat more confidence than he himself felt, and he decided that Wednesday's rehearsal would have to be even more intensive. The one thing he was certain of, though he couldn't say why, was that the girl had not dropped out, and that sooner or later she would be prompted to ask another of her devastating questions.

● ● ● ● ●

The next two days were filled with feverish activity, as The Unit, with its traditional cast, sought to make the production as foolproof as possible. Alan set aside his many other jobs temporarily to concentrate on the coming broadcast and booked extra time in rehearsal rooms, an unusual action which brought a few raised eyebrows. Everyone knew, however, of the coming visit of the *Look at Life* staff, and assumed that it was this that had The Unit jumping, a mistake that Alan welcomed and didn't bother to correct with even his closest associates. The newcomers were a bit startled by the amount of work required of them, even Jack Kirby noting that they had never made him sweat like this before—literally sweat, he commented at the end of one session as he wiped his dripping face with a towel. The extras finally concluded, with a grudging admiration, that if this was what it took to reach the top, then The Unit deserved every bit of its enviable reputation. Again, Alan didn't try to set them straight. He knew, as they did, that they had never worked this hard, and the experience would be good for them if they were serious about their profession.

In all, by broadcast time on Friday they were polished and flexible, and he was satisfied that they were ready for any possibility, no matter how far out it might be. The least talented of the extras was working weil over his head, and thoroughly savouring the feeling of being part of such a group.

Alan began by recapping the discussion at the close of the last lecture, evolving his own theory now that Shakespeare, the great economist, had made what amounted to a fortunate mistake in creating Falstaff. As he drew from his students the large number of functions that the fat knight performed in the play, it became clear that these would explain how Falstaff had grown to nearly unmanageable proportions and threatened to take over the play. To illustrate, Paul and Jack Kirby played several of the scenes in which Falstaff and Prince Hal appeared, and Falstaff, of course, became larger and more complex with each new function.

It was so good that Alan had virtually nothing to do to keep the class moving. The character of Hal himself was the next obvious subject, and Paul spoke his initial soliloquy twice, first showing the wild but honourable young Prince and second the egotistic, heartless, calculatingly honest plotter. Paul did so well that the choice was left wide open. As he moved through the play to Hal's victory over Hotspur and soliloquy over the fallen hero's body, themes emerged in sharp delineation, without a clear margin for either interpretation. It was perfect for the purposes of the lecture.

The students now pinpointed Act III, scene ii, as the crucial point of the play. Here, in the thematic climax, King Henry and Hal finally met, and Hal was forced to declare the purpose he had hidden for so long under his madcap actions. Ben and Paul took the two interpretations and ran them through. Finally a small but significant margin appeared, favouring the first interpretation, and Alan was about to cap it with Hal's final speech of the play when Merle, using a borrowed mike, hissed over the intercom, "Here it comes."

Instantly, Alan cut off the booth, throwing a glance at the two monitors. In almost the same sweep, he caught on both of them a glimpse of a girl with heavy glasses. As before, the voice came through like his, and he half-listened to the question while he brought both figures into close-up and debated wildly which of them it was. "These are the standard interpretations that have been accepted for years," the voice said, as he watched in vain for a sign of lip movement. "Isn't it possible, though, that Hal is completely unscrupulous and that King Henry has really—caught him with the goods, I guess you'd say—when he accuses him of being willing to turn traitor? Wouldn't he have to back off then and change his plans?"

Even as he struggled with his decision, Alan had to admit that the question was a very perceptive insight, and then, with a blinding realization, he knew which of the girls it was. The text! His vision last week had revealed a real text of *Richard II,* and one of these two had a solid, old-fashioned book on her lap. His gesture was almost casual as he switched the booth back in, split the screen, and cut in the girl.

"I'm sorry," he said gently, "but I don't think your question went to the other classrooms. Would you repeat it, please?"

There was a brief excruciating moment of dead silence, and Alan could see terror mounting in the girl's widening eyes behind the thick glasses. On set, Paul and Ben were looking to the booth, frozen into place. Then, with a gulp, in a voice trembling with fear, she began to speak. In her own voice, softer even as it gained strength than it had sounded when she had slipped a week ago, she put her question again. Alan picked it up, stressing its originality in a manner calculated to be encouraging without being overly flattering. He caught Ben from the corner of his eye, holding up thumb and forefinger in a circle, and without further discussion switched to the set for a test of the theory.

Immediately, he called Nick on the intercom and snapped, "Get Sam on to the instructor in the Miles City classroom. We've got to get that girl down here as quickly as possible. But for Heaven's sake, don't scare her to death. I thought she was going to pass out when she went on camera." On the master, Ben and Paul played out the scene according to the girl's suggestion. The rhetoric flowed on to a ringing, yet slightly false, climax. It was very plausible, very tempting, but despite the consummate skill of delivery it didn't quite convince. Alan eased into the concluding statements on the play without pressing the point, and was pleased to see that the girl was dispassionately jotting notes. It was over, or rather, it was just beginning he decided, as the broadcast ended and he walked down to the set.

Jack Kirby and the others were a bewildered-looking bunch.

"What was that all about, Alan?" Jack asked, but Nick interrupted with a quick: "Nice cover, Alan. I'll get the technicians to check out the circuits right away." Alan smiled innocently and Jack, after a quick glance at the confused extras, said, "Yeah, Alan, nice cover. Sure gave Ben and Paul time to reach for that far-out question." As the other men moved away, more or less convinced that they understood what had happened, Jack said in a low voice, "Whatever has been going on, I gather you've got it licked now. Do me a favour, though. If there's something screwy next time I guest, let me in on it beforehand."

Alan laughed weakly. "Jack, I promise you that when we do get it cleared up, I'll invite you out for drinks and tell you all about it. Thanks for giving me the benefit, and have fun back in New York." They shook hands cordially, and Jack left as The Unit gathered around Alan for a post-mortem.

Explanations took very little time, but quickly as they were given Sam was on the set with news. "Her name is Janet Ganski," he announced abruptly, "she's a second-year student, and she has reluctantly accepted an invitation to take part in a student-staff experiment being held here beginning Monday. She's been cleared from her other courses for an indefinite period, and her reservations are confirmed for Sunday. The suite next to yours is vacant, Sylvia, and because of the intimate nature of this, uh, experiment, she'll be moving in there instead of student housing. I expect that you, Olga, and Merle will make her welcome."

Continuing over the excited buzz, he spoke to Nick. "If you'd like to sign the papers in my office, The Unit can congratulate its new director. Alan, you have a brief to prepare for the new budget reporting on why a full director is needed for these courses, in addition to the senior lecturer. Now, Nick, can you introduce me to your temporary coordinator?"

He and Nick set off for the far end of the studio, while the rest tried to assimilate all the new information, and Alan fielded a host of questions. Then they retired to a business room in the cafeteria to plan for the coming meeting with Miss Janet Ganski.

Alan sipped absently at the coffee Sylvia had placed on his desk, while he checked over his work of the past few hours. It wasn't a masterpiece, he felt, but it would do if no one took it to bits in a close examination. He swung round and handed it to Sylvia. "Our application for the grant that Sam has already begun using," he told her. "An experiment in the use of a student consultant during production. To determine the value of instantaneous feedback. To determine the value of anticipating student reactions before broadcast. To determine the value of acquainting students with production techniques. And one or two minor areas of investigation. What do you think?"

Sylvia read it over, and gave it back with a nod of approval. "It takes a lot longer to read," she said, "but it sounds valid to me. You know, I realize that we're pulling a fast one because we're desperate to get hold of Miss Ganski. Yet I can't help wondering why no one has tried this before under normal circumstances. If I were on the Grants Committee, I'd consider this a brilliant idea."

Alan picked up his cup and left the desk. "I don't know," he answered, "but I'd guess it has roots back in the 1970s, when the students made their big bid for power in the old university system, and then abandoned the shambles they'd made of the whole affair."

"I've heard Ben talk about those days," Sylvia said, "and yet I can't imagine what it must have been like. I can't conceive of taking an undergraduate degree without those thousands of EVR courses to choose from, or not having had the best senior lecturers to listen to and work with for my master's."

Alan laughed bitterly. "You've had the best of two worlds," he said. "You got complete democracy at the undergraduate level, and complete autocracy when you proved that you could grasp the advantage of a system where you acknowledged your limitations, both temporary and permanent. We're lucky that enough of the old system survived the days of anarchy to build our present system on."

Sylvia looked bemused, and then shrugged it off prettily. "Well," she said, "I'm happy with my personal autocrat, and it seems that the students are happy enough with the rest. Meanwhile, let's talk about something I understand a little better. What can we do to make Janet Ganski's meeting with The Unit as painless and fruitful as possible?"

There was no doubt that all of The Unit were more than a trifle apprehensive about having a telepath on set with them. Alan was still seeking a plan by which she could be integrated without upsetting the cohesion of the group. As it turned out, however, the real problem was not in introducing her to The Unit, but in getting The Unit to function at all once Janet Ganski was among them. That very nearly brought total ruin on Monday.

There seemed, superficially, nothing outstanding about her when they met on Sunday afternoon. Average height and build, light brown hair and eyes, and potential prettiness, the sort that would need the right clothes and some help from cosmetics. If there was anything genuinely attractive about her, it was offset by the heavy, old-fashioned glasses. When Sylvia and Alan approached her, she emanated uncertainty and apprehension, and it was clear that she used the glasses as a shield from the world. They tried to put her at ease, chatting about her trip, her work, and the new experiment generally, but she remained much like some frightened animal, helpless between human captors. Nothing was said yet of her special talent, but they all knew that they would have to speak of it sooner or later, and it was largely this knowledge that created the tension between them.

Merle and Olga had more success making Janet intellectually, if not emotionally, aware that they were not about to put her through some brutal inquisition. In fact, Olga, with her special kind of compassion and outwardness, made good progress in establishing a "big-sister" bond, a phrase which she used when she and Merle reported briefly to Alan after the women had eaten supper in Janet's suite. Another thing which seemed to help was the comic confusion over ordering the meal. Janet had clearly been torn by a desire to be alone and the obligation to act as hostess, and something else as well. The others had simply ordered what they wanted, but Janet had hesitated, and settled for a cup of coffee.

It was when she took her AP Card from her carry-all that Sylvia realized what was bothering the girl. With a light laugh she said, "I suppose, like the rest of us, you'll be wondering how in the world you can spend all those extra credits you've got now. But even here, where there's not all that much to use them on, you'll soon start getting on to the blue, and maybe even on to the red. Right, girls?"

Janet blushed, and looked totally confused. "I thought," she stammered, "I mean—don't I just stay on the student stipend?"

"Not at all, Janet," Merle chuckled. "Everyone here gets forty per cent extra for skill participation." Janet's eyes grew big behind the glasses, and her blush grew deeper yet. Merle, who had caught the significance of it all, capitalized on the situation. "You're part of the team now, Janet," she smiled, "and we'll probably work you to death for your credits. But if you're here long enough you'll catch the skill work bug and be spoiled for anything else for the rest of your life." She put an arm over the girl's shoulder and added softly, "We think our group—The Unit—is something special, and we think you're special too."

She didn't pursue the point, but it wasn't lost on Janet, and the incident seemed to break down a bit of the barrier between them all. If she wasn't totally reassured, at least the girl seemed to accept them as well-meaning and friendly, and she relaxed enough to order a shrimp cocktail with a flourish of her "power card", as she called it.

Alan was tactful but frank when he dropped in later with Sylvia. Janet had been given a chance to rest and sort things out, and he felt that it would be pointless to waste time. He opened by telling her flatly that they had been interested primarily in getting her to Television Central on any pretext, and she reacted calmly but warily. Then he went on to say that the means which they had used were a sudden inspiration, but that they were genuinely concerned about using her talents in some way. Hence the reasons for bringing her might have been expressed rather vaguely, yet fundamentally they were exactly correct.

Janet had listened attentively, and now she spoke as openly as Alan had. "I just didn't think, the first time I asked a question. You see, I hate being out in—on display. I found out a long time ago that I could get other people to ask for me. But then it wasn't with people like you, just other students, and right away this time I felt I was making a mistake. I mean, it isn't just you, Professor Hamilton. Once I connected, if you can see what I mean by that, I could feel all the others in back of you. It scared me. More than all the confused thoughts and feelings that I've learned to shut out. And they were so bad when I was younger that I nearly had a breakdown once or twice. Exams. They were terrible, you know." She paused and hugged herself for a second, as if she'd had a chill.

"The second time, I didn't mean to at all, but there's something about all of you that's different. As if, when we touched the first time, it kind of fused or something. Now it's very easy to think to you. The question was asked before I could cut it off." She looked quite guilty at this point.

"I suppose that wouldn't be so bad," she continued, "but it goes through you, not only to you. I've never had that happen before, and I just knew that it caused a lot of trouble. There was a flurry behind you, like—like when you startle a flock of birds, almost. And I caught a hint of anger too. I would never have let you hear me again, if the third time I hadn't been simply too wrapped up in the book to realize

I was thinking 'out loud', and then it was too late, and I had made a mistake, and I was wide open for the backlash."

She kept her eyes down, fingering the hem of her tunic. Then she looked up with a timid smile. "That was probably my worst mistake, because the big feeling that came back at me was a kind of mixture of triumph and curiosity. It got me curious too, but I couldn't get up the courage to try it again until—until you put me right out in front of all those thousands of people. Honestly, I could have died on the spot. You don't know what it's like to have all those people touching you, as if you were in the middle of a spider's web." She looked straight at Alan, and suddenly he did know, graphically and shudderingly, and Sylvia jumped up and instinctively made a move to brush herself off.

"I'm sorry," Janet said breathlessly, "I shouldn't have done that."

"No," Alan said, "I think we deserved it. And it certainly was instructive." He glanced at Sylvia, who was cautiously sitting down, and she agreed fully.

"Anyway," Janet continued, "I might have just run away and hid if I hadn't already half-decided that I ought to be bold and take a chance. It's the first time anyone has really talked, thought, back to me. Oh, some people have reacted, the way you pull your finger back when you touch something hot. But someone deliberately thinking at me, *me!*" Alan had a frightening glimpse of absolute loneliness, of naked hunger for companionship, and then it was cut off.

"Janet," he said reassuringly, "I think you know now that we're all pretty reasonable in The Unit. I can't tell if we can give you all the things you need, but we're certainly not going to hurt you if we can help it, and we're vitally interested in finding out ways to use you in the group, not keep you quiet."

She gave him a warm, sincere smile and answered: "I think you all mean well, and in spite of a little reluctance I think everyone is trying hard to be at least scientifically neutral. One or two are a little worried that I might see things they don't want to show."

Alan was pleased that she had brought it up. "Tell me," he said, "how much control do you really have? For example, was the whole group feeling what Sylvia and I felt just now?"

"I don't think so," she said hesitantly. "I can control my 'sending' better than I can my 'receiving'. And I can't go into people's minds, though some are better at hiding thoughts than others. You people, for instance, seem to have a kind of circle that I can only get into by way of you, Alan." She looked quite wistful. "You share a lot of your ideas and feelings already, and the warmth and love among you is unbelievable. Like nothing I've ever known. It must be wonderful."

That was the substance of the evening's work. All three looked forward to the next day with mixed feelings. By morning, it developed, Janet had become so determined to be useful, to be wanted, that she tried too hard, and in so doing created confusion and near disaster.

Once the group were all assembled, they began to put together the first broadcast on *Henry V*. Janet sat attentively, listening and taking in a great deal. At the first break, however, when Alan asked how she was getting along, she admitted to being quite confused.

"You all understand so completely what you're doing that you move in jumps, and I have to piece the missing parts together. By then I've missed something, and have to catch up." Nevertheless, she kept at it when they began work again, occasionally taking a quick look at the prompt scanner, which Alan had been editing for snap cues as they went along. It was after they had settled the probable primary and secondary scenes and interpretations that real trouble began.

Nick had blocked in rough lighting and movements as they went, and now began shuffling hardware with the technical crew, while the rest of The Unit began doing lines. Janet was totally engrossed now, trying to follow everything that was going on, and obviously having difficulty.

On stage, Paul was doing Henry, while Ben did several smaller parts. Off to one side, the women were doing a scene at the French court. Nick was working with Ben and Paul, and shouting the odd instruction off into the gloom. " 'We are no tyrant, but a Christian kind,' " Paul declaimed, "swing the baby kleig to stage right." Nick looked startled, started to say something, and thought better of it. Ben frowned, Paul looked confused, but then they continued through the next bit of dialogue, until the point where Ben, as the French ambassador, was to present Paul with the contemptuous gift of tennis balls from the Dauphin.

He opened the chest with a flourish and sneered, " 'Alice, tu as été en Angleterre . . .' " then stood with mouth open as the women swung around to gape.

"Not fair, Ben," Merle called out. "Stick to your own lines."

And Sylvia said, "Make sure the casket opens to face bank two tricons."

Alan jumped, put both hands to his head and cried, "Hold it!" The

Unit seemed to realize simultaneously what was happening, and everyone tried to talk at once. "All right, all right!" Alan yelled at the centre of the confused group. "Let's try to make some order out of this." The noise subsided into uneasy silence.

"Now," Alan said firmly, "it's clear that we're getting crossed up with one another's thoughts. Let's find out what we can do to sort them out. It's Janet who's giving us the extra push, I think, so she'll have to help us get uncrossed. Janet!" he called, as he turned to look out into the darkness.

Off towards the studio doors there was a clatter and crash and Alan (with the others) felt sharp pain at shins and forehead, followed by brief vertigo. Olga swayed and reached out to Merle to steady herself, as Alan bolted off stage after Paul, who had already vaulted a chair and was dodging between pieces of equipment. When Alan got to them, Paul was already crouched beside Janet, holding an arm about her shoulders as she sobbed uncontrollably.

"I botched it," she finally managed to gasp out. "I botched the whole thing for you." For the moment there was nothing that Alan could say. He merely picked up the shattered glasses that lay in front of her, watched with compassion as she lifted a tear-streaked face and stared blindly at the blurred figures gathered around her.

● ● ● ● ● ●

It couldn't properly be called an argument, but the heated discussion that took place in Alan's office that afternoon was about as close to it as The Unit had ever come. The women were all for keeping Janet closely involved, even during the coming broadcast, while the men were more cautious, arguing that they couldn't afford a breakdown on network. Olga insisted that Janet had probably learned enough to remain aloof and simply watch, and Merle dismissed the importance of retaining perfection. "Everyone is entitled to a below-average shot once in a while," she said. "And if we mess up, you can cover for us with straight lecture, Alan."

Sylvia anticipated Alan's objections. "If we don't get her integrated now, we'll have to wait until the *Look at Life* crew is gone. It may seem like a short time, but it could tear Janet to pieces." Alan let them exhaust their reasoning, frustrations as much as anything, and then offered the only compromise which he felt was operable.

"We'll want to rig an observation area anyway, for the *Look at Life* visit," he stated, "and we need the adjustment to having someone in the studio if we're to perform up to standard. I doubt any of them will project the way Janet does, but if we can get used to her, then nothing should ever bother us again. Let's set up the area and put her in it. I have a feeling that she's going to be very careful from now on."

The others agreed to this. They split up, the men to work in a rehearsal room with the extras, the women off on some mysterious expedition, and Alan to revise his lecture notes for any emergency that might arise.

Late in the afternoon, Sam came in to check on their progress with Janet. He listened to Alan's account of the past two days' events with an air of deep concern, but agreed at the end that Alan's decision seemed the only workable solution. "I hope you don't drop the quality too much," he commented. "Rafferty is going to pick up something like that a half-hour after he hits the complex. There are enough rumours floating around here about you people as it is these days."

He prowled restlessly about the office, then moved close to Alan's desk. "Incidentally, speaking of rumours, I picked up a few more too. Don Scanlin and his wife seem to be in a stew about something. Had a big row in public at a Saturday night party. Don's been hitting the juice heavily lately too. The word is that his socialite wife is fraternizing with one of his crew over at EVR. Interesting?"

Alan chewed over the bits of information, but couldn't make them add up to anything concrete. "What do you make of it?" he asked.

Sam walked slowly to the door and turned. "I have a theory," he replied, "but I can't prove it now. Meanwhile, there's been no sabotage on your set for a while, so I guess we cross our fingers and hope. Tell Nick to be extra careful, though," he directed. "It would be murder if someone threw a wrench in the works while Rafferty was here." One more thing to worry about, Alan thought, as Sam left him to his lecture.

Tuesday morning opened with a pleasant shock for Alan and the other men. A grinning bevy of women entered the studio, shepherding Janet Ganski—the new Janet Ganski. She wore a simple tunic that hinted at a shapely figure which had been completely concealed before. Subtle makeup and hairdo had softened her rather blunt features and accented high cheekbones and dark eyes. The glasses were gone forever. She had been given a rush priority fitting for contacts. Now she stood in an admiring circle, self-conscious and girlish, but already beginning to acquire some self-assurance. Paul seemed particularly impressed, and it was more than professional interest that brought him back to talk to her during the pre-broadcast break.

The broadcast itself went far better than they had any right to expect. There were times when a faint stir of "alien" thought touched all of them, and they had vague hints of each other's concentration, but nothing more than that happened.

At the close, when Alan wrapped it up, a great wave of relief washed over The Unit, and Janet lay back in her seat and visibly went limp. It was clear that she had been exerting tremendous control and was totally exhausted by it. But she was just as obviously pleased with her effort, and accepted the compliments of the rest with a mixed eagerness and modesty. It seemed that they just might be all right from now on. Only Alan worried, for the moment, that this was in fact a quite negative relationship, and not at all what they ought to be working for, but even he was relieved that they hadn't been upset by complications. Let us get the *Look at Life* ordeal over, he thought, and then we can really come to grips with the integration problem.

Rafferty was thin-faced, long-nosed, affable and impish, and he had had one night to sniff around. He knew that some odd and interesting things were going on around Television Central, knew that The Unit was involved, and was practically bristling with invisible antennae. He had chosen not to meet any of the staff yet except Alan, but the two of them had hit it off well together, with the mutual respect of professionals. He sat in the observation area, and it soon became apparent that he had that knack for seeming to disappear peculiar to good reporters and pry-eyes. He had brought only one assistant into the studio, a tiny man who moved unobtrusively among the technicians and took footage with the smallest sound camera Alan had ever seen.

They spent the whole evening doing the usual workup. At one point Alan asked Janet's opinion on student reaction, and later Ben did the same. Her answers were direct and helpful and she became even more at ease with The Unit. They themselves could still feel, however, a tenuous but tough barrier most of the time, indicating that she was exerting a powerful control over her telepathic ability. On the rare occasion when she slipped there was a swirl of thoughts, from which they were forced to separate their own and try to hold on to them. It was a strange sensation, something like working one's own fishing line out of a tangle of several. The morning went well, and when Alan went to lunch with Rafferty the correspondent was impressed with what he had seen.

In the afternoon Rafferty's crew split up, one going with Nick, another with the actors, and Rafferty with Alan to his office for a brief period. They discussed the innumerable threads of production, the techniques of putting them together, and the little legman took some shots and went elsewhere. When Rafferty commented on Janet, it was merely to ask if this was usual procedure. His interest picked up when Alan explained that it was a new experiment, but he seemed satisfied with his own notion that The Unit would be a logical choice to try it out. Alan neither ducked the subject nor expanded on it, and they quickly moved to other matters.

Thursday was nearly a carbon copy of Wednesday, with The Unit moving to scene work, in the midst of lighting, costuming, props, and movements. Janet was there again, supplying a few more opinions during breaks, and much more comfortable with the hubbub and noise, hence much more in control of herself. Rafferty spent some time in the observation area, asked a few basic points of information from Janet about mid-way through the morning, and left. In short, everything was so natural and uncomplicated that Alan began to wish for a problem of some sort to shake them up a little. Nothing desperate, he hastily told himself, just a little problem to keep them on their toes. But it didn't come, and the day went by like a smooth-flowing river to its quiet close. An ominously quiet close.

Alan was a bit late in arriving at his office the next morning. Rafferty had phoned to ask a few last-minute questions, such as where his crew could monitor the broadcast, and whether his legman could film during broadcast, which Alan reluctantly allowed. He paused only to scribe a line in his notes, noted an urgent call from Don Scanlin, tried to reach him and couldn't, then headed to the bays. He checked the set and studio swiftly but carefully with Nick, saw the dim figure of Rafferty, caught a glimpse of Janet next to the prompt scanner, and slipped into the booth about seventy-five seconds before cue. All equipment working, notes open, and he was on, settling into the familiar routine and concentrating completely on the lecture. Two-thirds into the broadcast, all hell broke loose.

Not that they hadn't had warning, Alan realized, even as it happened. For some moments, unconsciously, he'd felt strain building, till the air was almost crackling. Then, with an all but audible snap, while The Unit was working over Act V, scene ii, all of them on-stage for the final scene in the French court, his mind seemed to open and encompass another half-dozen personalities.

There was Merle, mind crying out: "Up above! It's going to fall."

Almost instantaneously, Nick was literally pushing people into new positions, propelling them mentally.

Paul was speaking. " 'Now, welcome Kate: and bear me witness all . . .' " and on the line he swept Sylvia into his arms and moved forward and to the side. The others scattered in good order, and the co-ordinator found himself switching to a close-up of the Royal couple. " '. . . That here I kiss her as my sovereign queen,' " Paul finished, Alan cut himself back in, and one end of a long light boom came arcing down, chopping into the stage floor with a grinding crash, sending shards of shattered lenses and twisting power line through the space where most of them had been, from a dozen demolished spots and floods.

Through it all, Alan kept the discussion going, one part of his mind cool and detached, even as he felt the hysterical terror of Olga ebbing under the strength, calmness and comfort of Ben and Paul. Woven through the whole was a sense of bonding, of direction, of taut energy which Alan recognized as coming from Janet. He could feel that she was shunting some of the whirlpool aura from him, redirecting it to the others, and that she was somehow submerging her own personality to act as a kind of switching agent for the rest.

It was over quickly and The Unit physically huddled in front of the ruined set, when he felt them joining, thinking towards him as one, willing encouragement and warmth as he continued bringing students together, commenting, questioning, leading. There was wonder, respect and admiration, together with a great, tender regard for one another, and especially for Janet. Alan had never known such a command over his subject. He was working beyond his own abilities now, drawing unsuspected reserves from the whole of The Unit, even to details of information and insights previously buried within the group. His own sense of gratitude and admiration for the rest grew and spread among them.

Even as he brought the lecture to a close with an awesome summation, he was aware of a scuffle at the doors of the studio. Successive thrills of discovery, fright, accusation, disgust, and finally pity coursed through The Unit and lapped at the edges of Alan's consciousness as he visualized Don Scanlin, white, shaken, and desperately trying to explain something to an enraged Sam Meynard. The monitors went dead and he rose on leaden legs to join the group, only to find with a sense of overwhelming loss that he was suddenly alone again. There was a flickering sensation as one by one they all made distant contact, and when he reached The Unit the reason was plain. They were hovering over an unconscious Janet, worried and only vaguely aware of their own groping attempts to rejoin. Sam stood menacingly over Don Scanlin, sprawled in a chair with his long legs angled in front of the excited Rafferty, but Alan, like the rest, was only concerned for Janet.

It was an eternity to them before she stirred and groaned, then sat up dizzily. As she opened her eyes and looked slowly around in bewilderment, relief, love, and exaltation welled up and flowed over her to enfold her within The Unit. They were whole again in a way which made each a merged part, yet preserved them as separate and distinct. They could withhold or give what they wished, and they would have a long time together to adjust, to overcome a certain shyness.

Exhausted as they were, physically, mentally, emotionally, they gathered in Alan's apartment that evening to assess the fantastic events of the morning. Without exception, they had slept the afternoon away, though Alan had first finished his interview with Rafferty, and later Sam. He recapped the main points of the conversation. It might have been possible simply to open his mind, but they had already learned the tremendous toll it took to think so completely to one another. It was even harder without some problem or crisis as focus and catalyst. As yet, emotions and random thoughts passed among them without concentration.

Rafferty had got more story than he bargained for, and he was quivering with his desire to get away and work it out. He couldn't find enough superlatives for The Unit, and had actually stumbled after words to describe their reaction under pressure. "Never experienced anything like it," he had stammered. "Maybe during the Non-War. That smooth motion away from the boom that came down. Not a break in the dialogue, not a break in the action. My crew outside, watching the monitor cube, they never knew a thing had happened. Incredible!" Alan mimicked the correspondent's jerky gestures. "And that character Scanlin. Busting in with Meynard right behind him, and The Unit not caring a damn. Looking after the girl instead." He had gone on like that for some time, finally running down enough for

Sam and Alan to discuss how much ought to be revealed of Don Scanlin's part in the affair.

Sam had said what they all now felt, that Don had been guilty of enough to warrant dismissal, but he deserved some mitigation. He had been involved in the earlier attempts at sabotage, led by his own ambition and envy of The Unit and Alan, but it was painfully evident that Deborah Scanlin had driven him much further than he wanted to go. He had finally balked and she, with the help of the technician suspected by Sam and Alan, had plotted the last incident. It had been appallingly simple. He had slipped in during the night, wrapped several turns of soft solder round the bight of the end piece of strapping holding the boom, removed the nut and bolt, and left. He knew that the heat of the spot directly beneath it would loosen the solder. Whether it happened while someone was onstage, or before, seemed not to have troubled him one whit.

Deborah and Don had got into a roaring argument at breakfast and she had produced her great coup with a disparaging tirade. Don, horrified, had tried to reach Alan and then raced for the studio while Deborah, wisely, had left hurriedly for a vacation—somewhere in seclusion. Rafferty was for releasing all the details, until Sam tactfully brought up the matter of her family's holdings and influence. The correspondent still obviously ached to write the whole truth, but he reluctantly agreed that his editors would surely suppress it, considering the magafax's shaky finances. At the end, the three men had parted on excellent terms, Rafferty still singing the praises of The Unit.

Peace and gentle satisfaction permeated Alan's suite, as the couples sat together talking quietly. Ben and Merle, Nick and Olga were in a far corner, planning a joint trip to the Bermudas for Christmas. Sylvia and Alan were watching more than talking, comfortably settled in the usual place on the low couch before the window.

"Well," Alan heaved a deep sigh, "I'd say we made history of some sort today, though not many people would understand it, even if we could explain it."

Sylvia snuggled close as she answered. "We'll probably make a little more history before we've finished too. It's going to be mighty interesting developing The Unit's new talents. Janet is nowhere near her full potential, I'd guess, and that probably goes for all of us. I only hope she'll stay."

Alan gave a knowing laugh and nodded towards the closed window and balcony. "She'll stay," he chortled.

Out on the balcony, absolutely oblivious to the fact that they were coatless in a growing curtain of drifting snowflakes, Janet and Paul were enclosed in their own world. Sylvia placed her hand in Alan's and murmured, "That's good. So good for both of them." Then she sat up straight and hugged herself. "But darn it, I wish they'd come in. *I'm* freezing to death."